Null and Void

Books by Lewis Ashman

Fiction:
October

Poetry:
Possible Worlds
Love and Other Wrongs
April Fool

Null and Void

*To Donna
best wishes!
Lewis Ashman*

Lewis Ashman

Rev. date: 05/18/2018

To order additional copies of this book, contact:
Xlibris
1-888-795-4274
www.Xlibris.com
Orders@Xlibris.com
778354

Special thanks to
Karen Batridge
for editorial help

I'm scared of that child
I'm scared of that child
I'm scared of that child
Because I'm too young to die

—Sonny Boy Williamson

1

Lance Thompson arrived at the north end of the high school parking lot sauntering along as if he was just a casual good citizen out for an indifferent evening stroll. The moment he had returned to his room after finding out his brother had been beaten up, he had shot out of the window and started toward the school. He passed through the night woods easily, down through the park, a trail he had walked so often that finding his way through the dark was no problem at all. There was a light rain, and the occasional lights reflected and glittered on the grass and road like the infinite stars; it was like walking through a galaxy. He smiled at the idea and trudged on for the school by back streets, not wanting to have anything to do with the police. It was very late for a fourteen-year-old boy to be out.

Stanley Wilson and his friends were lolling about on the fenders or hoods of various cars, if anything even drunker than when they beat up Lance's brother, Mike. There were maybe twenty of them all together, a few athlete types and their girlfriends, a few unattached girls looking for attachment or just passing the time, all of them more or less drunk and all of them except Stanley smoking cigarettes, though Bob Farrell and Huston Smith were puffing on small cigars in a show of phony and ironic elegance. They were talking loudly or singing along with one of the car radios turned up loud. A couple of girls were dancing.

Lance strolled directly toward Stanley; he was the toughest of the lot, the biggest and strongest, and the only one who actually knew how to box. It would be best to confront him first. Lance walked down quietly at a steady smooth pace, and finally Stanley noticed him and lurched up from the fender he was almost lying on, throwing off his suede jacket and swinging his arms like some kind of ape.

"Well, if it isn't Little Thompson." Stanley's words were slightly slurred. He leered at Lance with a weird sort of joy. "You know, we kicked the hell out of your clown brother tonight."

"Yes, Stanley, I already heard about you beating my brother up tonight. I heard all about it."

Lance didn't say anything else but only looked steadily at Stanley as he walked on directly toward him. The kids in the parking lot quit talking and began to smirk and give one another looks, watching.

"I suppose you think you've come to settle things up, you lil twit."

Stanley lurched a step toward Lance, but Lance was already right in front of him. Without saying a word, Lance fired his right fist directly at Stanley's throat, just below the chin; and Stanley's head cracked back, his neck spraying blood. Stanley dropped like a chopped-off tree, and the back of his head smacked the pavement with the sound of a watermelon breaking into shards and water.

Bob and Houston dropped their cigars and lunged toward Lance. Lance curved his left fist around into the side of Houston's head, crushing the wall of his skull, and Houston dropped to the ground like a broken doll. Lance's right fist struck Bob just behind the ear as Lance's left leg swung underneath him and tripped him. Bob's face struck the asphalt dead on and broke like another dropped watermelon.

Andy had climbed out of the backseat of a car where he had been making out with a freshman girl he didn't know, and he was just starting to move toward the fight, such as it was; but as he saw how things were developing, he turned and ran across the football practice field. Lance started after him; but Hank Henderson, a tackle from the football team, jumped in front of him, shouting, "Whoa, boy!" Lance struck him firmly twice, left and then right, squarely on the chest; and Hank's sternum snapped, and he fell to the ground, screaming. Lance looked, and Andy was already at the end of the practice field, vanishing into the pines.

Lance turned and looked at the crowd. The girls were screaming and crying; the boys were running around and shouting and waving their arms in the air. Everything had turned into a rushed cacophony of disaster. Doug Anderson, who actually liked Lance, stood perfectly still, his eyes wide and enormous, surveying the bloody bodies. All three of the boys Lance had first hit were obviously dead. It was impossible. You couldn't just kill someone by hitting them once or twice. But there they were. It was impossible, but there they were. Lance stepped up to Doug and said, "You tell Andy I'll catch him later." Then Lance walked off north out of the lot, heading toward the wooded park and the path through the dark. He shook his arms, and sparkling drops of water flew into the darkness.

Lance had always been a difficult child, a baby who didn't want to sleep, who was moody about eating, veering from self-starvation into gluttony, a toddler who would gurgle around happily and then suddenly start screaming for no apparent reason. Something no one else could see or sense was completely terrifying him. He was a challenging child who seemed to be from another world. At around ten, he started complaining about stomach pains; and his folks submitted him to a doctor's care, which meant a stay in the hospital for a battery of tests. No particular cause for stomach pains was ever found, but some anomalies in his digestive system were observed that might at some later date cause him problems. Surgery was the best course of action, so the doctors said, though it wasn't clear exactly what the point was.

And so at twelve, Lance was subjected to a six-week summer stay in the hospital, undergoing major surgery and then vital treatment for the infections that resulted from the hospital staff's collective incompetence. They never seemed to get things quite right. It seemed to his father, Alex, that Lance had become addicted to whatever the pain medication was that they were giving him in such liberal doses mostly, Alex thought, just to shut Lance up. He went from crying that he needed a shot for pain to crying that he needed a shot—he just needed a shot. After his shot, he would settle back into wakeful rest, usually singing some sort of nonsense over and over. As Alex sat beside his bed reading Dickens (not too difficult to read but interesting enough to pass the time), Lance would lie in bed and say things again and again, once repeating the word *pumpernickel* in various tones and volumes until Alex was tempted to slap him. He didn't, but he was tempted. He considered asking that the boy be given even larger doses of pain medication, enough to put him out cold, but that seemed like a reckless and excessive response to what was mostly just Lance boring his father.

Eventually, science triumphed, and Lance was sent home more or less recovered from whatever the anomalies were that weren't even bothering him. And yet he was never the same. He was a peculiar sort from the get-go, and his hospital stay only made him more peculiar; in fact, Lance became downright strange. Taken in hand by his big brother, Mike, Lance began a program of weightlifting so that the kids in junior high, and by implication Mike as well, wouldn't think he was a sissy. Lance seemed to become quietly obsessed with his workouts, not only lifting enormous amounts of weight every day but running for miles out along country roads with weights attached to his ankles. Mike's weightlifting hadn't done much for him in terms of appearance: he was still lanky and slender, though much stronger. Lance, on the other hand, blossomed into the full look of a passionate bodybuilder. And he kept at it every single day with a determination that seemed pointless since he had no interest in athletics.

Other than building a beautiful body, Lance's strangeness became manifest in a variety of ways more or less unavoidable to the rest of the family. He became a careful picky eater, picky to the point Alex had to say repeatedly, "Eat your food, Lance. Don't dissect it." But Lance went on pulling servings apart with his fork and staring into them as if looking for something. Otherwise, Lance became silent and withdrawn, though given to staring at anyone who talked to him with a puzzled investigating look, as if wondering who or even what was talking to him and why they didn't just be quiet. Eventually, the family more or less quit talking to him; his fierce questioning gaze was just too weird to suffer through merely to get the corn passed or find out what the weather was like. What did Lance do? Other than lift weights and attend school, he read his way through piles of books, he played war games by himself in his room, he studied chess books, sitting in almost absolute stillness with a book propped open in front of him, the pieces in a frozen array before him. He pondered. He thought. He would go into the yard and sit in a chair, very still, and stare out into the forest. Stillness. Thought. Meditation? Sometimes it seemed like meditation or a nap, but more often it seemed like he was waiting for something. Or someone.

Every issue in the Thompson family eventually touched on what might be called the Lance factor. Buying a car or planting a garden or pruning the trees or planning a vacation always at some point came down to the question: "What about Lance?" The whole family was essentially frightened of Lance. How would he react? What would he say?

Generally, Lance didn't do or say anything in response to the family. He lifted weights, he ran, he read his books, he thought and sat, he played his games, and he waited. The Thompson family activities seemed far away from him; his attitude was sort of like Alex's pastime of watching birds on the lawn; curious fellows those birds—what are they doing now?

And yet even his detachment made the Thompsons nervous. There was always the possibility he might say something or might even do something. Mike would rant and complain and protest when the family was making decisions, but that was accepted by Mildred and Alex and even Mike as just the squeaky noise of a teen trying to get his way. It didn't amount to much, and eventually the family would do whatever Mildred thought best. The only woman in the family, she had the gender card to play, the manners card, the deference-to-the woman card; and it was the joker in the deck—it trumped everything. They would do what Mildred said, but they were always afraid of what Lance might say or do. Even Mildred was afraid.

After he beat those boys to death, people had good reason to be afraid of Lance; and he was handled by the police as if he was a dangerous adult killer, not just a rowdy juvenile delinquent. He was held in a cell by himself, and when he was moved from room to room to talk to various investigators, it was always with him cuffed and accompanied by an armed guard. And yet the usual legal form and order for teens had to be observed, and that meant an interview with Michelle McKinney.

Michelle had a job to do like anyone else, but most days she didn't think it was much of a job, certainly nothing to get excited about. She had majored in clinical psychology in college mostly because she was interested in how the mind worked, but she was only mildly interested in troubled minds. Or even other minds. Mostly she wanted to find out what made her own mind work—or not work. She wondered mostly about herself. She probably should have just gotten a degree in psychology, but she was nervous about getting a job. A degree in psychology would have been about as useless as a degree in philosophy when it came time to seek employment. So she added the clinical aspect of her degree during her senior year when she went into a sort of panic at having to face leaving college. She had consoled herself with the notion that she might actually help people. Of course, she wouldn't be an actual psychiatrist, but she could listen to people and counsel them gently to find a way to live productive and happy lives—maybe. What had never particularly been about other people turned into exactly that.

Her job wasn't much in the way of counseling or helping. Most days it seemed that about anyone who could read and write could do her job. She was listed as an assessing counselor for the Youth Services Division of the criminal system, attached in some fuzzy way to both the courts and the office of the county prosecutor. Which meant, oddly, that she had a badge on her ID. She wondered if it would get her out of a speeding ticket, showing her ID and having that badge right there; but she drove carefully and never sped, so she never found out. Her job was to interview little criminals, as she called the troubled youth who were her clients, by using an enormous form of direct simple questions. At the end, there was a single page for her personal handwritten observations, but it was clear to her that no one read that part; the powers above her just wanted the questions asked and the answers tabulated and filed. Did it make any difference? Not that she could see. Her forms were shoveled away into the system, and she never heard about what she had done again. She was never called to testify in court or answer questions for lawyers. For no specific reason she could say, she suspected that the forms she filed were only used for population descriptions and had no real effect on any particular case. She went through the motions and collected her check, and it was okay but not especially rewarding or meaningful. Just a job.

She sat in her tiny office assembling herself for her first client, absentmindedly shifting forms and papers across her desk. She was an attractive slender vaguely Ukrainian woman with a head of hair that was just there, clean and combed but just there. At one time, back when she first went to college, she had tried various styles and haircuts; but it always seemed to end up that she was just a woman with hair, nondescript and without particular form. Maybe it was dishwater blonde. If she spent time outdoors in the summer, it would start to actually look blonde but anymore she hardly ever spent time outdoors. She just went to work, went home, read her newspapers and books, and tried not to think. Her face was oddly perfect to the point that people would sometimes give her double-takes, the glance followed by a stare. She wasn't strikingly beautiful—she wasn't beautiful at all. But her nose, eyes, mouth, and cheeks were all perfectly in order, perfectly proportioned. She looked like an ideal Greek sculpture of a woman's face, perfectly proportioned but oddly lifeless and slightly cold.

Aside from her papers, her small desk had two pictures. One was a professional studio shot of her mother and father. Often such pictures only show a bland resemblance to their subjects without carrying over much of their personalities; in this case, Michelle thought the photographer had captured her parents perfectly: two old folks looking pleasant and bland but somehow nervous and on edge, as if they were leaning forward slightly in an anxiety of uncertainty and self-doubt. Yes, that was Mom and Dad.

The other picture was a small print she had clipped from a calendar of Mary Cassatt's painting *The Boating Party*. To Michelle this was in some way the greatest painting in the world though it wasn't really great in the sense of grandeur or imposing majesty. The scene seemed common enough: a woman holding a child and a man rowing the boat they were all in, a broad stretch of lifeless blue water, the angling away white, almost gray, sail. The man in dark clothes, the woman fashionably overdressed, the baby fat and pink—and smiling. The colors were fine and almost meticulously balanced, broad angles and geometric forms. It comforted Michelle to look at it; she liked its balance. She was in the habit of seeing it as her father rowing and her mother holding her, a flashback into an impossible past of her own family. Of course, the woman didn't look at all like her mother and the dark bulk of the man could have been anyone. That didn't much matter, and yet there was a more profound problem, and this was what really gave the picture its allure for her. Michelle would look at the painting as a painting of her family and yet be sure, be certain, that someone was missing. Somehow the picture was incomplete. And that air of incompleteness drew her into looking at it steadily in wonder and curiosity. A wonderful, graceful, but frightening picture.

Today she would be assessing Lance Thompson; she had her white lab coat on, and she had a clipboard with her pad of questions, and she was wearing her Buddy Holly hide-your-face glasses. She looked vaguely professional and vaguely scientific. The boy in question, Lance, was a fourteen-year-old who had beaten three larger and stronger boys to death with his bare hands and then crippled a much larger boy by breaking his sternum. He had also threatened "to get" another boy. Glancing at that, she concluded he was some kind of monster. He would be restrained at the table in the examination room, and an armed guard would be present, so she probably wasn't in any danger. But it made her nervous to have to deal with such a violent character. Normally her clients, the little criminals, were car thieves or drug users or simply kids who wouldn't go to school. This was a rare case—an actual pathology. And yet it was part of the system that she had to interview every single adolescent who was held and charged with a crime.

He was sitting quite still at a wooden table in the clean white examination room, staring up at the ceiling in a gaze of mild concentration. Ed Morgan, the usual security guard, was standing off to the left with his hands folded in front of him, and he nodded pleasantly to Michelle as she took her seat. She smiled back and then looked at Lance. He diverted his gaze from the ceiling and looked directly into Michelle's eyes with a straightforwardness that at first startled her. And yet Lance seemed harmless enough, only looking at the ceiling, looking at her. Then Lance smiled a little.

"I noticed that the ceiling tiles are alternated in their patterns so even though they're all identical you can see a chessboard arrangement if you focus on it that way. I was playing a game of chess. I was winning."

"Weren't you playing both sides? No matter what, wouldn't that be a draw?"

Lance gave a quick smile. He was an ordinary-enough-looking boy though one who had done some serious weightlifting and one who had more than the usual teen acne. Michelle looked up at the tiles; and yes, there was a grain in each tile; and yes, they did form a kind of chessboard pattern in the way they were arranged. But.

"I don't believe you were playing chess on the ceiling in your head. You're trying to impress me, and you're not impressing me at all."

Lance sat very still as if she hadn't said anything but then slightly nodded, affirming.

"I'm Ms. McKinney, Lance, and I'm pleased to meet you. I have some questions I would like to ask you."

"Aren't you going to tell me you're Dr. McKinney? You might as well since your name isn't really Michelle McKinney."

Michelle tried to maintain her professionalism, but she was pretty sure she had rolled her eyes involuntarily. She focused on setting her features firm.

"Excuse me, Mr. Lance Thompson, my name is McKinney, and I am not a psychiatrist, so the doctor address would be inappropriate. I only have a bachelor's degree."

"Whatever."

"Why don't we begin?" Michelle placed the clipboard in front of her, rustled the pages forward past the detailed forms she would fill out later, and turned to the first page of questions.

"The strangest thing about me isn't that I killed those guys. That was just a fluke. The strangest thing about me is that I know things."

Michelle stopped rustling her pages.

"It was just a fluke that you killed those boys? Explain please."

Lance shrugged.

"I hit them, right? And I hit them hard because there were so many of them and I had to move fast. I didn't want them to all fall on me at once, and I certainly didn't want to make a fool of myself by losing the fight. So I hit as hard as I could and as fast as I could."

Michelle waited a couple of beats. "And?"

"Well? Suppose you hit Ed here"—and Lance nodded toward the security guard who ignored him—"suppose you hit Ed as hard as you could. Do you think he would die?"

"No."

"Okay. So you're me. I hit those guys as hard as I could because they beat up my brother, and I wanted to punish them, and I sure didn't want them to beat me up. I never dreamed I would kill them any more than you would kill Ed here by hitting him as hard as you could. It was a fluke, a weird fluke."

Michelle nodded. "Uh-huh. And do you feel bad about it?"

Lance seemed to think for a few seconds. "No. I guess I don't. It seems like I should feel bad about it, but I really don't care, which is kind of strange."

"No doubt. I would be miserable if I just broke someone's sternum and put them in the hospital, let alone killed three people. There's something . . . different . . . about you."

Lance shrugged.

"Why don't we get to work on these questions, Lance? There a lot of them."

"Don't you want to feel my head for lumps?"

Michelle couldn't help grinning. "Phrenology is not a sound science, Lance."

"Is psychology?"

Now Michelle shrugged. "That's an open question, I guess. But unlike phrenology, psychology has proven over time to help some people. Phrenology never helped anyone."

"You're in an abusive sexual relationship."

Michelle didn't move, struck breathless by what Lance had said, though she colored quickly deep red. She had an urge to slap him.

"Your husband hurts you during sex."

Michelle glanced away as she raised one hand slightly from her papers, a vague gesture.

"Your crystal ball is cloudy, Lance. I'm not married. And by the way, my name is still McKinney. For someone who claims to know things, your average is pretty poor."

A look of genuine perplexity crossed Lance's face. He gathered his brow into an image of deep concentration and briefly looked down at his cuffed hands on the table.

"You have a boyfriend. It was okay at first, but then he started to want weirder and weirder things. Now he hurts you."

Michelle rolled her eyes intentionally this time. "You always end up right with your 'knowledge,' don't you? Even if you have to change it in midflight, so to speak."

"I'm always right at the center. Sometimes the peripheral details are a little off. Sometimes the details are exactly right. When I play my war games, I have to resolve battles by rolling a die. Usually I have no idea what the number will be, but sometimes I'm absolutely certain. And when I'm certain, I'm never wrong—never. If I know it will be a three, then it's a three. Always."

"Have you ever had sex, Lance?"

"Me? No. I'm only fourteen."

"Right. So you don't know what you're talking about. Even normal sex has an element of abuse in it. You just don't know."

"Oh, I know enough. We had sex education in school—twice—and I've read things, heard things. I have a pretty good idea what happens, though I can't imagine me ever doing such a thing. I mean, having sex actually happen . . . it seems impossible."

Michelle nodded. "That's how I was at fourteen. I thought I knew about it, but I couldn't imagine it being done to me."

Lance smiled. "'Being done to me'? I think we're reaching the core of your problem."

Michelle gave an exasperated little smile. "But alas, we're not here for my problems. We're here to find out about your problems."

"I don't have any problems."

"Said the killer."

"As I believe I explained, that was essentially accidental."

"That's your story? Good luck with that. I think you're looking at spending the rest of your life in various very uncomfortable institutions."

"Oh no, no no. They can't hold me here. I'll be free in a few days."

"Oh? More of your 'knowledge,' Lance? You keep thinking that way, and maybe I'll come visit you when you turn fifty. I'll bring you some killer cookies."

Lance chuckled lightly. "You're funny, Laura, but you're not hilarious."

Michelle raised her eyebrows. "Laura? Your 'knowledge' is perfectly awful. My first name is Michelle."

"So you think."

"Well, I would know, wouldn't I?"

Lance gestured toward the guard. "Let's talk about Ed here."

Michelle gave Lance an exasperated grimace. "Let's not, Lance. Let's get started on these questions. And by the way, his name isn't Ed Here. Your knowledge continues to be lousy."

Lance brushed her comment aside with both hands and went on, turning and speaking to Ed, who appeared to have not been listening at all. "You have a niece Claire, right?"

Ed raised his eyebrows but nodded.

Lance closed his eyes and began to speak slow and low, not quite imitating a charlatan performing a séance but certainly resembling it, even if unintentionally. He seemed to be at once summoning knowledge and showing off. "Little Claire has a growth behind her right ear, which is getting bigger. It's not dangerous now, but it needs to be looked at. If it's removed promptly, she'll be okay, but if it goes on growing, it will be bad news, big trouble later."

Ed seemed to soberly consider what Lance had said. "Well, I'll take a look next time I see her. You got her name right, so I'll look."

"At the cookout Friday? She'll be there."

Ed nodded. "Yes, we're having a cookout Friday and she should be there. I'll look at it, and if you're right, I'll tell her folks."

Lance looked at Michelle with a casual gaze of accomplishment. "Ed believes."

"Sure, Lance. Now these questions. Let's get started."

"Why don't you believe?"

"Oh, I believe, Lance. I believe you know everything only not quite accurately."

Lance shook his head fiercely. "No, no, I never said I knew everything. I just know some things, things there's no plausible reason for me to know."

"The questions, Lance."

Lance closed his eyes and went into his routine again. "You were born Laura McGovern. You have a twin sister, Rita. You were born out of wedlock. Your mother, Cheryl, knew she would have to raise her babies alone because your father was merely a ship passing in the night. She couldn't face raising twins, so she put you up for adoption."

"Right, Lance."

Lance opened his eyes and looked at her directly. "Come on, Laura. Think about this. You know, you've always known you have a twin. You know your parents aren't really your parents. You know I'm telling the truth."

"I don't know and haven't always known any such thing," but her voice was quavering doubtfully.

Lance closed his eyes and started again after a brief pause of apparently seeking knowledge. "It's, um, 1024 Brookville Road in Burton, Ohio. Burton isn't much, just a crossroads, so it will be easy to find. Your mom and sister are living there. Look them up."

Then, with his eyes open and a gentle smile, "Look them up, Laura."

His bout of visionary knowledge over, Lance had relaxed quietly into the mind-numbing task of answering all the questions on Michelle's form, questions that were no more interesting to Michelle than they were to Lance. Michelle had never developed much of sense of what all these questions were aiming at or what they told anyone, but it seemed to her that Lance had answered them about the way any average fourteen-year-old boy would answer them. Then Michelle gathered her papers and left. She hadn't seen him again, and as these things usually went, she never would see him again. She wasn't actually treating him. She was just part of the process of assessing him.

No doubt about it, Lance had struck a bare spot in Michelle's personal armor. The boy was outlandish and absurd in his claiming to have special knowledge, and yet for all his fumbling around, he did seem to be able to weirdly summon up facts he couldn't possibly know. Ed's niece, for example. It could be nothing, but Lance had nailed enough of Ed's situation that it did make it seem that the boy had some supernatural access to facts. The abusive husband or boyfriend he ascribed to Michelle's life was completely inaccurate, though she was as uneasy about sex as anyone. Her experience was far more limited than Lance gave her credit for. But her occasional dalliance in lovemaking certainly hadn't been wonderful: pushy sweaty boys in the back of cars treating her like a pleasure package they could have their way with. They seemed to enjoy it, but Michelle thought it was awful, something to just get through. She wanted to have a social life like other young people. She wanted to have boyfriends. But an oaf who barely knew her name groping her in the dark was anything but romantic, anything but human.

It was a puzzle to Michelle why life moved the way it did and things didn't happen that were supposed to happen. Judging by novels and TV shows and, yes, Hollywood movies, she had everything available to her during her adolescence and early twenties that any other girl had. She should have been able to construct a reasonable facsimile of the usual life: various boys experienced to various degrees leading into her settling on one who actually liked her and so having a steady guy and maybe after a couple of steady guys moving on into marriage. And children. And perhaps some miraculous feeling of love that would complete her life and hold everything together in a pattern that was whole and made sense. Something magical. Something that gave color and luster to the plain this and then that of daily life.

But boys continued to be blandly horny in the most indifferent and coldest way, and Michelle lost interest in even trying. She would go to a movie or dance at a party with a boy or later with young men, but almost subconsciously she angled herself away from getting caught alone with any of them and being expected to feel what she didn't feel, expected to want what she just didn't want.

What she wanted was peace. She wanted the broken part inside of her healed into a unity. She amused herself at life and found her own pace and her own direction, diligent at her school work and relaxing with corny television or movie fantasies of life as someone else thought it could be. The real curiosity for her was why she was so unsatisfied; what was it in her mind that made her conclude that something was missing? She gravitated into studying psychology because her own brain was such a mystery. She didn't consider herself one bit mentally ill; she assumed that she was boringly typical except in the aspect that she wouldn't settle for less than it seemed should be real. Her parents loved her almost to suffocation, but they were raising her to release her; it came up again and again that she would go away to college, that she would have her own place, her own life, whether it included a man and children or not. Her parents loved her and wanted her out on her own. But Michelle didn't feel complete on her own. In some basic way, something was missing. She felt strangely like everyone else had another hand that she couldn't see or another set of legs. Everyone else was fully equipped for life, but she only got half the kit.

When the boy took his shot in the dark and prophesied that she had a twin sister, it immediately made sense to Michelle. That would explain everything even if the boy didn't really know what he was talking about half the time. The fact that he could give her an address and names—it made it seem almost real. If she had a twin, if there was another her whom she had been separated from at birth, maybe that would explain everything. "That would explain everything" became like a hard piece of wood that Michelle couldn't stop chewing on. Maybe her emptiness and her detachment and her feeling of being lost had a perfectly natural physical cause. She felt like only half a person because she really was only half of two people who should have been together.

Immediately after her interview with Lance, almost against her will, Michelle had called her mother, the woman she thought was her mother, to get the facts.

"Mom? It's Michelle."

"Oh, hi, honey, your dad is out dusting the roses. This is the worst year ever for Japanese beetles. I don't know why we don't just give up. I'll go get him. He'll want to talk to you too."

"No, Mom, I just want to talk to you."

The phone was dead, so she concluded her mother had gone to get her father, which wouldn't make this any easier. Michelle drummed her fingernails on her phone table.

Her dad's voice came over the line, "Hi, Michelle, boy, this is a wicked year for bugs. I've never seen it so bad. The garden is looking good, though, even though it's a battle. We've got tomatoes, of course, and peas and onions, and your mom put some spinach in—"

"Mom and Dad, I want to talk about something important."

Both voices chimed in, "Oh, honey, what is it? Are you okay?"

"I know this sounds really weird, guys, but . . . was I adopted? Did you adopt me?"

Michelle heard a firm click on the line. Apparently her father had hung up.

Her mother's voice came on in a subdued, sober tone, "Oh, Michelle, what are you talking about? You know your dad and I are your parents. We raised you since you were a little girl, a tiny baby."

Michelle's heart sank clear beyond the floor. She felt vaguely like she had been hurled into outer space, and there was nothing to breathe, nothing to see but stars spinning wildly in the endless darkness. Her mother filled her in with brittle sad assurances of all their love, her adoptive parents' profound love. But what Lance had said was essentially true. She was adopted, and her real name was Laura, but her mom and dad had changed it to what they liked, Michelle, so she was really born as Michelle into their family, the family of three. Mrs. McKinney didn't know anything about her birth mother, and she had never heard anything like that Laura might be a twin. Laura, no longer Michelle, got off the phone as quickly as she could. She curled into a ball on the floor and cried for longer than she had ever cried before, but she didn't really know why. It felt good to cry is all. Her parents had been wonderful, really, and she had been happy. It shouldn't matter, but somehow it did matter. The lost spot inside her that had flavored even the nicest days might, in fact, be her twin, Rita. It made sense, but it was only partly good news. Mostly it was disconcerting. Mostly, it was sad.

And so Michelle, now Laura, was on the road through the fall fields of Indiana to Burton, Ohio. She chewed on the name Laura and decided she would accept it, but it took some thinking about, some consideration. Changing your name, your identity, all at once was a disturbing and unsettling chore. And that, the name, was only the smallest part. She couldn't decide if she never knew who she was or if she knew but hadn't faced it or merely hadn't had proof of it or if, maybe, it all was just a bad dream that would go away, go away.

Laura circled back to thinking of Lance and his mysterious impossible knowledge as she made way through the crackling Indiana cornfields, the landscape at once harvest and emptiness. He had only been the instigator of her movement, the change in her life at hand; and at this point, he was essentially a distracting thought, a diversion. But for Laura, the facts of the case, which was her life, were just too much to face steadily. Somewhere in the east, she would arrive at a house and there meet the woman she didn't know, who was her mother, and another woman she didn't know, her twin sister. If asked, she would have said nothing was more important to her than her family, and yet now it turned out she didn't even know her family, not her real family. She would say, if asked, her real family was the couple who had raised her, Mom and Dad with their roses and garden concerns and endless love and support and encouragement. And yet in some strange sense biological and yet more than biological, these others would be her family as well. Or perhaps instead, though that felt like an impossible thing to grapple with.

The road unwound steadily, a white streamer of concrete under the direct Hoosier sun, only bending occasionally away from some ancient form of enormous trees or a house the highway department decided to build around instead of over and through. Wooden shingles on the wall of a barn, a strange witchcraft sort of design painted underneath the hayloft. Four horses running in an empty field, circling back just as Laura flashed past. A sort of river or stream almost without water, more the bed of what could have been a stream but only seen for a moment, Laura driving on, steady and level.

And then a town out toward the Ohio border and Laura driving aimlessly into the center and beyond, circling back a block from the main drag, huge oaks and maples shading the streets, broken in places into a few sad blocks without any cover, dry weeds jutting up from the sidewalk concrete. Empty stores. Bare windows. The dust of fall and curious distant light, direct but somehow turned aside, and the bare sky empty and blue and deep. Laura's radio was on; but she wasn't listening, tapping in time on the steering wheel with her fingers even when she didn't hear, not with her mind, the music that enveloped the inside the of the car. Radio reports came and went, and perhaps she heard them on the surface; but her thoughts were never focused directly only flitting from detail to detail, the broken shutter on the library window equally significant to her strangely overturned sense of herself, who she was, her life.

There wasn't enough in the town to hold her, and eventually Laura had to go on into Ohio. As she had been told by Lance, supernatural Lance, Burton, Ohio, wasn't much more than a crossroads and 1024 Brookville Road was easy to find, a slapped-together board house that had seen careful maintenance and perhaps paint at one time but was now a dusty-looking shell leaning a bit in places where a house was supposed to stand straight. Masked from the road by a line of worn and misshapen cypresses, Cheryl McGovern stood square in the center of a block of grass and violets and clover, her lawn, spraying with casual indifference great arcs of water from a brass nozzle she held loosely in her hand. Even from the car, Laura could see her features clearly: a middle-aged woman of solid build whose face was gentle and wrinkled with grandmotherly softness and care. Her eyes were bright and like Laura's perfectly slate blue.

Suddenly it was all too much for Laura, and she went into a panic, the air in the car close and small. She clutched herself tight like a fist. She knew who her parents were, and she knew who she was; and this woman gingerly tightening the brass nozzle and shutting off the water, looking at her with a half smile at once perplexed and mild, wasn't her mother. Laura held tight to the wheel, spinning a bit and slightly out of breath. How awful. How awful.

And then she was out the car door and up the gravel drive, pausing to stand and look at Cheryl, full in the face, direct, her feet moving her somehow forward. Cheryl's smile stretched full.

"Why . . . it's my baby, girl."

Cheryl dropped the hose, crossed her arms loosely over her belly, and stepped back a bit on her left foot as if to give herself room to give Laura a good look.

Her smile was enormous but her eyes sad.

"Now look here. I know you've got questions, and maybe you think you've been done wrong, and maybe none of this makes any sense . . . but come give your momma a kiss."

Laura was cradled and held and squeezed gently but firmly against the round soft bulk of her mother, touched directly on the lips briefly by that happy mouth, and then held at arm's length, tears everywhere from both of them, though they were quiet.

"Oh well, Laura, I didn't pick you and I didn't pick Rita. You girls were as alike as those two buttons on your blouse. I didn't pick at all. But I couldn't take the both of you. I just couldn't be a momma to two, not without any help at all, so one of you went and the other stayed. It just had to be that way, but it doesn't mean a thing. I love you both exactly the same. Always did. Always will. I've thought about you . . . my—"

"It's okay, Mom. It's okay."

Laura looked past her mother, and there on the crinkled white-and-gray boards of the porch stood a woman who might be Laura herself; so exactly did she duplicate her, she might have been a mirror image. Might have been that is if Laura had an arm folded aside awkwardly like a broken wing, or stump stumble of walking with one leg slightly shorter than the other, or finally if Laura had had an enormous white wound like a jagged edge cut by a saw across her face, just missing her eyes. Laura stared and tried to take in the image of herself, her twin, damaged terribly but exactly there, on the porch back behind Cheryl.

Cheryl noted Laura staring and turned to look herself, quickly all in a glance, taking in the hurt young woman. Cheryl stepped back from

Laura as if to give her a clear look and waved vaguely toward the house. Cheryl leaned forward and spoke quickly in a soft whisper, though the woman on the porch was too far away to have heard her very well even if she'd yelled.

"That's your sister, Rita. She had an accident. She was just like you before, but you can see she's been a bit mangled. It's been hard for her, you being such pretty girls and all. Yes, yes, my"—and Cheryl sighed expansively before calling out, "Rita! Hey, Rita! Come on down here and meet your sister, Laura."

Rita didn't seem to hear, or she heard, but she wasn't in much of a hurry. She paused at a bowl of petunias and began to distractedly pluck at the blossoms, pull at the leaves.

"Laura's come to visit you!" Cheryl called out. Then she fell back into her conspiratorial whisper, "Well, she was with her husband, John Thomas, and the two boys, Will and Gerald, and they were coming over a hill in a rainstorm. John Thomas always drove like he was in the biggest hurry in the world, you know, always had to be there quicker, and well . . ." Cheryl looked at Laura, waiting for a response.

Laura tapped her mother's arm and looked at her directly before gazing back at Rita. "Yes, Mom, what happened?"

Cheryl sighed again. "Well, there was a big fuel truck sprawled all the way across the road, and they smacked into it just like that, just like that. No time hardly for John Thomas to even hit the brakes. John Thomas and the boys were killed outright, but by some miracle, Rita pulled through. She's not been the same, though. I mean, it isn't just her looks that have changed. Think of what she's lost!" Cheryl stared at Laura almost with an air of accusation.

Laura took her mother's arm, and they started walking toward the house, Laura pulling at her mom gently and saying, "Oh, terrible, terrible, poor Rita. That's just awful, Mom," which seemed to satisfy Cheryl that Laura felt bad enough.

Rita leaned lightly against the post of the porch and gave Laura a wry smile as she approached. "Hey, sis . . . look at you." And Rita stepped toward her.

Again Laura was enfolded, though this time by the near-stick figure form of her sister, hugging fiercely and yet briefly, only to step back, each of them, holding both hands and looking. Rita's eyes were charged and delighted, staring directly into Laura's; and Laura knew she was looking back at Rita, into Rita, with exactly the same passionate directness. It felt, Laura thought all at once, like being home. It was her sister, her sister.

It was an odd but beautiful confusion they settled into. Cheryl had drifted off, and it was just Laura and Rita sitting together on a collapsing sofa under the front-room window, staring at a huge print across the room of ducks flying over a pond, cows standing near the water, a covered bridge over the stream flowing by, a barn in the distance, all of it some kind of conflation of every detail of the nature of mixed wood and fields of a typical country scene, typical to the exaggerated point of being strange. Then looking back at each other, snapping into smiles and bright eyes, listening and talking, holding hands. Comforting.

They gradually sank into each other the way a holy man deeply meditating would sink into himself: conscious and yet unconscious, letting everything easily and simply be and flow, in and out, the happening ease of pure existence. The usual border Laura had always felt between herself and everyone else, the line where Laura ended and the other person started, vanished entirely with Rita. She knew that anything she said would immediately be understood, and yet even further there was so much that could be left unsaid that was being understood, moment by moment, exactly herself reflecting exactly into herself until she didn't know at all, or care, where Laura ended and Rita started. There was only one—Laura and Rita, Rita and Laura. They were together.

Off in the kitchen, not seeming to know what she was doing and yet cleaning and straightening with precise hands exactly handling everything, Cheryl couldn't have been happier if she'd found a million dollars waiting for her in a bag at the end of the west field. This was what needed to happen, and it was happening just so. It seemed forever that Cheryl had wrestled with her regret at having let Laura go. Back then, what did she know? She liked men. She liked having a good time, of a sort. She didn't even know which man was the father. The man didn't matter. He was just a spasm, his spasm, her spasm. Cheryl smiled to herself; yes, she liked a good time then, of a sort.

But then, when she discovered she was pregnant, it was time to be different, to make right choices and be adult, use clear judgment. She was going to be a mother, and she certainly wasn't going let that make her have a man around all the time. Men had their place, but she wasn't going to live with one. All she could see was what an enormous job a baby would be, and two babies—that would just be too much. So she thought. But mere weeks after she'd let Laura go, Cheryl knew she had made a terrible mistake. Babies were work, yes, but they were also beautiful blessings, and to have had two would have been all the more wonderful. She had fallen in love for the first time with Rita; she adored Rita, every little fingernail and elbow and eyelid. She wanted Laura back; she wanted the both of them—her girls. But it was too late.

Cheryl sighed as if it had just happened, a deep resounding sigh of regret and acceptance both rolled together into a puzzled abeyance of judgment, her usual mode for facing what she had done. Maybe. That was where she lived. Maybe.

2

When Happy Wilson graduated from high school, the only thing he knew for sure was that he was going to be a scientist. It was a curious ambition. Looking back, he realized that he wanted to be a scientist about the way a five-year-old boy wants to be an Indian chief. He had some sort of a notion of a guy in a white lab coat who knew many things and could talk at length about complicated issues while carrying a clipboard. Maybe some test tubes, maybe a bubbling flask on a black workbench, some hoses and vats and peculiar smells. A scientist. A respected expert who . . . did things.

It didn't work out that way. Happy had almost no interest at all in nature, and he was at best an indifferent math student and a thoroughly doubtful biology and chemistry student. He kept clean and precise notebooks. He did that. He organized things without really thinking about it; he seemed to have a natural flair for lining up tables and facts. He could see when things were out of place. It wasn't much to build a career as a scientist on.

At college he did okay but only okay. Computers fascinated him with their ability to call up virtually any fact at all and offer a system for placing it in harmony of a sort with other facts. He had no interest in how computers worked, and programming was completely outside his area of ability or focus. But he liked using computers. And when the internet blossomed, he knew where he belonged: looking things up. Almost without seeing it, he slipped from being a biology major to being a paralegal major. But who wants to work with lawyers all day?

To work in a law office and have a lawyer for a boss? That sounded like hell to Happy.

Somehow he stumbled into being a private detective. He had never even considered that as a career, not for all the years he muddled around at a variety of unsuitable jobs, but that's what he ended up being. If he had thought about it, his notion of a private detective would have been based on old movies and detective novels. Carrying a gun. Drinking whiskey. Philandering with loose women. Gunfights in dark alleys. But his actual job of being a private detective was nothing like that. He looked things up, mostly. Sometimes he interviewed people, but that was merely a process of getting more facts; he hardly ever had anything like a verbal confrontation, let alone a fistfight. He would assemble a file folder of papers answering the questions he'd been hired to answer and he'd turn it over to his client who would walk off with it, and that was that. It was about as romantic and exciting as being a bookkeeper.

Happy knew without reflection that he was an odd duck. It didn't bother him particularly, but he knew he was peculiar. Other people had childhoods of varying degrees of happiness and misery; other people had tortured or splendid adolescent years they could recall in passionate detail. To Happy, it seemed he had been born an adult private detective. It was a biological certainty that he had had parents, but they were dead now. It was a biological certainty that he had had a childhood, but what was it? What was it like? What happened?

Not much that he could access. He had a fairly precise memory of standing in front of a motor lodge at Mammoth Cave bathed in sunlight and smiling awkwardly, but really, that was just a memory of a photograph that was probably in a drawer somewhere. How could he have an actual memory of seeing himself? No, it was just a snapshot probably taken by his father or mother, dim characters he could remember clearly but not really so clearly, not really. Mammoth Cave itself he remembered only as a park ranger standing beside a floodlit rock wall talking about something, some geology thing, and how boring it was. There must have been more to it than that, but he couldn't remember. Similarly, he remembered being on the USS *Constitution* running his hand along a large wooden beam and hearing a young naval cadet of some sort going on at endless length and with an incomprehensible accent about the features of the ship. Or so he supposed. So he had gone on some sort of vacations with his parents, family trips. And he had gone to school . . . he supposed. Not much of a childhood. Probably happy. Okay.

Then adolescence. Other people could talk at length about love or sexual exploits or drunken rampages or academic achievements or sports or clubs or . . . or whatever . . . but all Happy knew for sure was that he must have learned to drive and it must have been during his teen years. That was when people usually learned how to drive. He had no clear memories of any particular classes or any friends at all. Little moments would surface in his mind, like being nervous doing a math problem at the chalkboard or talking to someone outside the school and not understanding what they were talking about, but there was no narrative, no story to Happy's adolescence or childhood. He was born an adult private detective.

At some point in his adult life, Happy quit boiling an egg in the morning and instead started having his breakfast at the Spotlite Diner. The Spotlite was a 1930s house with a 1950s box tacked on the front that had the diner counter in it. A narrow pole barn shape had been added in the sixties with seats around circular tables. All this was painted bright white with angular green stripes, an apparent effort to draw these disparate architectural shapes into some kind of a unity. The whole thing was plopped in a field of corn squeezed between the river road and the river, a field that frequently flooded. For no particular reason, the Spotlite sign featured a huge ice cream cone; their actual business was focused on root beer and burgers. You had to be careful, though: they had a tendency to put peanut butter on things you wouldn't expect peanut butter to be on.

Marge seemed to run the Spotlite, but she may have only been the manager of the waitresses. It was hard to get a clear bead on what the setup was. She hardly ever waited on anyone in the mornings, but she would hustle around checking stock and poking into things, supervising the two women she called her right and left hands. It was easy to see which woman was the right hand and which was the left. Laura was quiet and friendly and efficient and moved with easy grace from the coffeepots to the counter with the plates of steaming eggs and hash browns and on out to the customers, quick but never flustered and never appearing to be in a hurry. Rita, who seemed to be her sister, was somewhat slower and more prone to distraction. She had a slight limp and seemed to have a problem with one of her arms, and her face had a jagged white scar—damaged goods. She was just as friendly as Laura and in some ways even nicer since she would linger with a customer and not let herself be rushed from one to the other. Rita never let being busy get in the way of a good conversation.

One morning there was no one in the Spotlite except a gray businessman in a gray suit off at the other end of the counter. Happy ordered his usual hash browns and egg over easy, toast with mixed fruit jelly, bacon, and hot coffee with a glass of water. He sort of ordered. Laura jotted down what he wanted more quickly than he talked, so he guessed she remembered that he always ordered the same thing. Marge was nowhere around; it was just Laura and Rita, and really Laura could have handled everything. It seemed Laura and Rita were a team; they always worked together even on mornings like this when there was barely any business. The Spotlite was known for their root beer and burgers, not their breakfasts.

This morning Laura was keeping busy in her level, calm pace, but Rita drifted over to chat.

"Hey, Happy, how's the snoop business?" Rita flashed him a smile and then looked off toward the hills outside the window, the high bluffs of maple over the river.

"Secrets everywhere, Rita."

"You gonna catch the bad guys? Or just shoot 'em?" Rita grinned.

"Heavens, Rita"—and Happy's hands fluttered over his half-eaten breakfast—"you know I abhor violence."

"Uh-oh. No movie about you."

"That's fine. I don't like too much attention."

Rita raised her eyebrows in mock judgment. "Well then, I'll leave you alone with your breakfast."

But she didn't move off. She only stood and stretched and continued to look out the window.

Happy poked at his food and tried to think of something to say. Talking to waitresses was essentially his complete social life. It wasn't a big deal, but it was his main human contact. He liked to talk with them. They were people, but they didn't much matter. It was easier than most social interaction.

"Mostly I just do background checks these days. Nothing very exciting." Happy paused. "Do you know, Rita, that some people lie about their past? They do."

"I'll bet. But tell me why."

"Well, there are things they don't want other people to know, like that they never actually worked at such and such a company or never paid off such and such a loan."

Rita looked at Happy as if assessing him.

"Happy, how do you know when you know something?"

"Well, hmm." Happy looked at Rita, and Rita looked directly back. Apparently she really wanted an answer.

"I know I know something when I find a record of it, a file with the facts written down. The things I need to know are always recorded somewhere. If they aren't recorded, then I can't know them, not in the way I need to for my job."

Rita gazed off at the floor.

"Whatta yuh know, Rita?" Happy tried to imitate a casual greeting.

"Not much, Happy." Rita smiled. "What do you know?"

"Loan defaults." They both laughed.

"So you're like a historian."

"Yes. A personal-history historian. Though I don't have much personal history myself."

Rita grinned. "I'll bet. You're probably one of those quiet types with a dozen bodies buried in the crawlspace."

Happy laughed and said in a fake ominous tone, "You never know, Rita. You never know."

Rita folded her arms in front of her and leaned on the counter.

"Here's what I mean, Happy. I didn't know I had a sister"—and Rita nodded toward Laura, who was filling napkin dispensers at the other end of the room—"until recently, but I sort of knew I did. I mean, I could feel that someone was missing who was supposed to be with me."

"Well"—and Happy moved on gingerly—"after the accident, I'm sure you feel like people are missing . . . people *are* missing."

"Well, sure," Rita blurted out, "of course, *those* people are missing. I feel like my personal history is over, all done, everyone gone. But even before that, I felt like someone was missing. I thought about it a lot. Who is missing? And I think I decided that I just wanted to be married, that what was missing was a husband and kids. And that was fine, you know. I loved them all, but none of them were the missing person."

Happy nodded and said, "Right," but he obviously didn't get it.

Rita sighed. "It's like this, Happy. You come in here and you want something and you order eggs and it's good and you order hash browns and it's good, but somehow it's not what you wanted. What you wanted was a hot fudge sundae with nuts and a cherry!"

Happy bowed his head as if he was suffering. "For breakfast, Rita? A hot fudge sundae?"

"Why are you tormenting this man?" Unnoticed by either of them, Laura had walked up behind Rita.

Happy spread his hands toward Laura. "And here she is! Your hot fudge sundae!"

Rita and Happy laughed, and Rita put her arms around Laura. "Yup. Here she is, nutty as all get out."

Laura laughed and shook her head. "You guys are crazy." She walked off toward the back.

"So how did I know, Happy?"

Happy was putting money down on the counter and getting up.

"Well, you didn't know. You just had a feeling. Now if you hire me, I'll go look up the birth record. There's almost certainly a birth record, and I'll make a copy of it and give it to you, and then you'll know that you know that you have a sister."

"Jeez, Happy, thanks a lot. For money, you'll tell me I've got a sister when I know I have a sister. I can touch her and see her. She looks just like me . . . except," and Rita gestured away.

"Similar, sure. But you won't know you know until I do the paperwork."

Rita shook her head.

"Have a good weird day, Mr. Detective Snoop."

Happy went out to the Spotlite parking lot and climbed into the flight deck, as he called it, of the Exploder. For three years Happy had driven a tiny Chevy with rear-wheel drive that hardly seemed to hold the road even when the weather was excellent. Given the least ice or the wind of a passing truck, he could barely tell where the Chevy might end up. He had driven through an ice storm once and seen half a dozen cars just like his off the road stuck fast in snowy ditches. He was a careful driver, and he managed to stay safe, but driving the Chevy was frightening, a little car that carried him low to the road and couldn't manage any serious speed at all.

So he went to Crane's Used Cars and bought the Exploder. It was almost a truck. He got a good deal on it with an undercoat thrown in, but in the case of the Exploder, the undercoat was a bit late: rust damage had driven holes into the hull of the Exploder somewhat like battle damage in a World War II bomber. But Mr. Crane assured him in his loud expansive way that painting the underside now had stopped the rust in its tracks, and the touch-up of gray that covered the car's wounds gave the whole thing a spirited look. That's what Mr. Crane said, a "spirited look," and Happy had no clue what he meant by that; but he accepted that there was some core of wisdom at the root of it. Happy knew nothing about cars. To Happy, the Exploder was a box on wheels that had about as much spirit as a box on wheels could have, a plain old box on wheels.

Happy did know and enjoy the fact that driving the Exploder was a whole different brand of experience than driving his tiny Chevy. The wheel base was wide; the seats were up high, perching him vertical instead of slouching down like in the Chevy; and there was power to spare in the huge motor. With the push of a button, the Exploder would go into four-wheel drive, which seemed to mean something though Happy never really figured out when he should use it. Happy thought that it would only be helpful if he was actually driving through snowdrifts or river mud, but there was almost surely more to it than Happy knew.

At first he kept careful track of the Exploder's mileage, but once he realized he would never get more than seven miles per gallon on the highway and considerably less in town, he lost interest in his facts and figures. It had a big tank; and he just filled it up, standing for a much longer time at the pump than anyone else, whistling thoughtlessly, and gazing around at the landscape. Now that paying for gas was essentially a credit card deal, he could cheerfully run twenty-plus gallons into the Exploder without ever looking at how much it was costing him; he disciplined himself not to look at the money end of keeping the Exploder moving. And the Exploder did move; in fact, it roared. Happy loved the feeling of perfect safety the Exploder gave him. Even the noise of it was comforting.

The Wilson Private Investigations office was hidden away in a long two-story brick building filled with the offices of dentists, realtors, financial consultants, tax attorneys, and even a fortune teller of a sort, Madame Helene's Future for You. Or partly filled—many of the offices were vacant, and the largest advertising sign for the whole building was a giant For Lease billboard that looked flimsy and temporary but had been standing for five years out beside the highway. Happy thought it made the whole concern look like it was failing, and maybe it was. According to his lease, Happy was supposed to get cleaning of his office, cleaning of the general hallways, and a thorough attractive grounds maintenance. Not much came of that. Someone swept the stairs and hallways once in a while, and occasionally the lawn of dandelions was mowed; but the flowerbeds had all gone to weed, and the handsome ornamental trees hadn't been pruned in years. Winters saw the parking lot and sidewalks choked with ice and snow.

Happy clicked the lock open with a special sort of twist of his wrist that he had mastered, which was the only way to get the lock to work.

Everything inside was exactly the same as the day before, exactly the same as every day. His computer monitor was front and center on his desk, surrounded by a slovenly jumble of loose papers. His wooden armchair that slightly reclined and eagerly turned with the least push of his toe to the floor had rolled back against the wall when he sprang from his chair at exactly five and left work for the day. A couple of stiff dining room chairs were across from his desk against the far wall—seats for clients, though almost all of Happy's work was done by phone and computer anymore. It was very rare for him to even see the people who hired him to check out the background of their prospective employees or borrowers. Off to the left, he had his personal water closet, and he supposed the trash was overflowing there just as it was in his office proper. It was his own duty to empty his trash, or so it seemed. No one else was going to empty it.

Happy sat down slowly and clicked the computer on. Waiting, he tipped back and looked out the window where he could see nothing but a clear blue sky. Eventually a bird flew by. Otherwise, he might have been staring at a plain blue concrete wall. From his chair, he could never see anything but the sky. It gave him the feeling at times of working in the top turret of a castle, the fabled ivory tower. But his work was hardly intellectual and not at all philosophical or artistic. He accessed records and made copies and poked around for more records. Work that used to require going to various county courthouses could now be done almost entirely by computer. Happy sighed and reflected for the hundredth or so time that he might as well work out of his home. He didn't need an office to do research on a computer. And yet it seemed to be some sort of wisdom to keep his occupation separate from his domicile—that is, his seedy little apartment not all that much larger than his office. Its only distinguishing feature was the twin bed against one wall and the kitchen corner with its stove, a half-refrigerator he had to squat down to look in, a stained steel sink, and an equally stained yellow Formica table that could seat two but never did.

For perhaps the hundredth time, Happy gazed at the print hanging on the wall opposite his desk and wondered if he should replace it. It was a large somewhat water-stained print of Mary Cassatt's masterpiece *The*

Boating Party stamped out on a huge piece of cardboard lightly textured with random swirls to, Happy supposed, resemble paint brushstrokes. Happy had never seen the original, but he was skeptical that it was anywhere near as large as his print. In his tiny office, it looked almost like a mural. He certainly loved the picture, but was it right for the office of a serious businessman, a private investigator? Happy had very little to do with women and nothing to do with little babies; but he liked looking at them in the picture, all dressed up in an old-fashioned style, heading across an incredibly blue lake in the nicely bowed arc of a white boat. He was curious about the boat being propelled both by a sail, completely white, and the huge figure of a darkly dressed man rowing who, to Happy's way of thinking, was facing the wrong way. But of course the woman and child were in the back of the boat. The rower was facing the right direction, but the point of focus was not the direction of the boat's motion but rather toward the woman and little girl. Happy always had to straighten that out in his mind when he studied the picture, which wasn't often. It had hung there forever, and he had meditated on it probably for hours when you added all the minutes together; but really for days at a time, he never even glanced at it. It was a sign of how long he had been there, leasing that same office, that he could have thought so much about something he barely looked at. When he did look at it, he always imagined himself to be the man rowing. And the woman and the child—he shied away from trying to figure out who they might be.

Perhaps a print of a clipper ship would be better, all sails and spray and waves, lunging powerfully across white-capped water with threatening clouds looming behind, or maybe that old print of a McCormick's reaper standing solid and strong in the center of *The Battle Of Shiloh*. Happy always liked that picture, smirking at the absurdity of it as an advertisement. But. It was time to get to work.

Happy was very good at his work and completely focused on it; he lost himself in the minutia of finding appropriate files and records, assembling them, organizing them in just enough detail to get the facts across without swamping his client, and then writing the brief summaries that he suspected were all his clients ever looked at, the summing up and conclusion of the story the records told. He never thought about the people involved as actual people; the notion of the actual people was irrelevant. What mattered was how they appeared in their documentation; for Happy, that was who they were. He would putter along at his work like this at a steady speed, accurate but not quick, until it was five. He would barely pause for lunch, eating a granola bar from his lap drawer in a sort of honorary salute to lunch at exactly twelve, but mostly Happy just worked away. His work suited him, and it supported him, simple and direct.

Slightly more than halfway into the day, there was a sharp rap at his door that startled Happy so much he wasn't sure it was real. He paused with his hands poised over his keyboard and stared into the middle distance. There was another rap at the door, and Happy could make out the dull silhouette of someone standing outside the milky glass.

"Yes?"

A boy opened the door and stepped in, glancing around the office. He was well built, obviously a weightlifter, but his face had a pinched hungry look, and his darting eyes were filled with anxiety. He was not exactly filthy, but he was unwashed. He carefully clicked the door shut behind him and stepped up directly across from Happy.

"I need your help."

Happy pursed his lips and gestured toward one of the chairs. The boy pulled it up so his knees almost touched Happy's desk when he sat down.

"How old are you, son?"

"My name's Lance. I'm sixteen."

"Generally my clients are grown-ups."

Lance shrugged and raised his hands. "I can't pay you, so I'm not really a client."

"Well, what do you need?"

"I need you to find somebody for me."

Happy eased his lap drawer open, took out his last three granola bars, and extended them toward Lance, saying, "I'm a private detective, but I don't do much in the way finding people, and I never do anything without being paid. You can eat these."

This last wasn't really necessary. Lance had immediately taken the bars and peeled the silvery paper off one and promptly started munching.

"Where are your parents, Lance?"

Chewing furiously, Lance made an empty gesture away. "My parents are irrelevant to my life."

Happy nodded. "That's not an unusual position for sixteen-year-old boys to take, but I really think you should probably be with them. I'm sure they're worried about you."

Lance kept munching. Then as he peeled another bar, he responded, "Maybe."

"So where are you from?"

"I just got here from Chicago. I had to see somebody, take care of something. Before that—" Lance waved aside vaguely with the granola bar he had just started.

Happy sighed and looked around the room. "So you've been on the road."

"Well, a day in Henderson, Indiana—that was . . . pretty exciting. Terrible really. Awful."

"Henderson? North of here? Not much in Henderson is there?"

"Not much. Less since I was there."

"They had a bunch of shootings there, somebody wiping out the crime I hear."

"I was there. Then Chicago and now I'm here to see you."

"I can't help you, son."

Lance stopped eating for a moment, pulled up in his chair, and began addressing Happy somewhat more loudly and emphatically, "Listen, I know things. I know things there's no possible way for me to know. I know you can help me find Laura and Laura can help me. I've got to find Laura, but for some reason, I can't find her myself. You know where she is. It's not a business thing. It's just that I know you know where she is, and all you have to do is tell me, and then I'll leave you alone." Lance slouched down and set to munching again.

Happy leaned back in his chair. "Laura."

Lance kept eating, and Happy's eyes scouted around the room, touching on the woman in the boat. "Are you . . . on drugs?"

Lance peeled the last of the granola bars. "No. I don't have any drugs. I wish I did. I'd sell them and buy cheeseburgers."

Happy leaned forward. "I can't help you with this Laura person. I—"

Lance went into his loud and emphatic voice again. "Yes, you can. You can help me. You know where she is. I'm sure you do. Just tell me—"

"Steady. Steady, Lance. Don't get riled."

Lance leaned back in his chair, fingering the flimsy wrappings of the now-vanished granola bars. "Thanks for the food. Here's the deal. Her name is Laura McGovern, and she has a twin sister, Rita, and she lives somewhere in this town. I'm sure of that."

Happy pitched himself forward in a loud fake sneeze and felt around for his tissues. He was completely surprised to realize that he did know where Laura was, surprised and amazed and maybe a little horrified. But there was no way he was going to tell this boy where she was. Not at least until he talked to Laura. If then.

Happy stood up, dabbing at his nose with a tissue. "I have to work, and you have to . . . go do whatever you do." He moved to the door and pulled it open.

Lance stared at him and then rose slowly, edging toward the door.

Happy fished a twenty out of his wallet and handed it to Lance. "Suppose I find this Laura person. Should I call you at your office maybe?"

Lance flashed a grin and took the money. "Don't worry, I'll be in touch. Thanks."

And out the door he went. And Happy shut the door and sat down and looked out the window and sighed.

3

From the white broken concrete slab on which she was perched, Cheryl McGovern looked out over the landscape and worked steadily at puffing on a Marlboro, a habit she should give up but there it is, there it is. She was perhaps a hundred feet from the rail line, a double strand of I-beam shapes rusting somewhat black and red but shiny as a new knife along the tops. The tracks appeared to be set atop a long mound of ground coal. The roadbed was that black. Even the ties were black as if smeared with tar, though in places she could see bits of very dark and very worn wood, not quite natural wood somehow but wood.

It was a solemn and genuine satisfaction in Cheryl's life to sit out like this looking around at everything and waiting for the train she knew would be along in ten or so minutes. She often came out to look at the trains, to watch them pass by, and to listen to their powerful lurch and squeak as they rose and fell and pushed on forward, swaying a little, appearing to sway a little, at the curve just beyond where she sat. She knew there were other people—men mostly, mostly old men—who liked to watch trains; and they were usually experts of some sort, men who studied trains assiduously and could go on at boring length about schedule tables, engine types, car types, train designs, and train history.

Cheryl had little in common with them. She didn't need to know anything about trains; she just liked to be there when they went by, to smell them and hear them and feel their power as they found their way along. She even liked the sort of back of the city landscape where the tracks were laid. It seemed to Cheryl that many people talked about loving our beautiful world, but really, what they loved were calendar pictures. The sun setting over a tropical lagoon, a rocky mountain peaked with snow receding away over a small perfectly blue lake, a hill of maple trees in their brilliant autumn red and gold: calendar pictures of nature, generally without any sign of people or even any sign that people lived on this earth, in this world.

It wasn't like that for Cheryl. She loved life. She loved being alive. She sat on her perch of crumbling concrete and inhaled the day, the presence of the day and her sentience of the day, as if it were the smoke from one of her cigarettes. She was, she existed, and she could absorb and revel in the sensation of being. There were the train tracks, and she could see them, and she could smell them; and if she held still and didn't think, it would begin to seem that she was them and they were her, everything around passing into and passing out, freely being as she was freely being.

Yes. She said yes to everything. And if it was dirty and it was human and it was worn out and broken, well, it was. Litter didn't disturb her. The caked crusty white plastic containers and the tiny slips of scrap paper and the blowing thin plastic bags—they just were, and she was there and she took them in quietly and she let them out quietly. The worn ground around the train tracks and around the surrounding wrecked buildings that had once been some kind of factory or business or busy concern of some variety of long gone people, the ground of all that had once been as natural as the rich cool dirt in her flower garden, the dirt she loved to clench in her fingers as she pushed it aside to carefully place a flower. This ground, the train ground, had been that; and in time it could be that again, perhaps. But it was what it was, and it barely resembled her garden; but still, it was what it was, a gray ashen drifting dust or the hard-packed almost-rock soil pounded by moving heavy vehicles, spotted with rocks and pieces of rocks and bits of broken glass and the black mysterious forms of some kind of tar, the salamander shapes of the black whatever it was that had cooled into a soft misshapen something unnatural. Still, it was there. And Cheryl looked and accepted without discriminating, and it was lovely to be there, to be alive and simply let everything in and everything out.

There were plants. Even in the broken railroad factory ground, seeds found their way, a few seeds, a few plants, found their way to root and grow and extend the small fabric shapes of leaves, of spikey hard stalks, and eventually after inexpressible struggles to even flower. Cheryl thought of a poem she had read once, read a long time ago and perhaps not read well, not with deeper understanding. It was a poem by Jack Kerouac or Allen Ginsberg or one of those guys, a poem about a sunflower blossoming beside a locomotive. She didn't remember the details, but she could recall the form of it, the shape of the direction of the thought, and the poem seemed as she recalled it to be saying there was some kind of contest between the industrial and the natural and it seemed to be sharing the hope that the natural would triumph, eventually. Something like that—Cheryl wasn't sure.

But it wasn't like that for her. For her, there was no triumph. Or rather, simply being, existing, and being aware of existing as deeply as possible was already a triumph. The victory was won over emptiness and nothing and the despair of not knowing. A person could know where she was, and a person could love knowing it. A person could look around and see. And smell. And feel. A person could be.

Cheryl looked around again, not discriminating; and suddenly she was amused to see that she also had sunflowers, three of them, pushing up from the grit and grime, the dirt of the world and the dirt of humanity, three tilting long stalks with withered leaves topped by the crowns of those over-large flowers, almost too much for the stalks, each with a halo of gold petals like yellow flaps and a center of seed like a honeycomb pattern of black and white. Sunflowers. Who knew how they got there, but there they were.

And there were other flowers, more common, the little networks of slender branches reaching out to tiny white or blue blossoms, extended shrubs as high as Cheryl's waist. Or the single dandelions golden and perfect or gone to seed white and puffy and, yes, still perfect. Broad-leaf weeds apparently without any flowers that looked like plants from the floor of a jungle back in the days of dinosaurs, a single strand of seed standing straight up like a mast.

Cheryl simply sat, not even waiting. The train would be along sometime. This was what it was, and it was good. She scuffed at the white concrete with her tennis shoe, knocking loose a couple of gray pebbles and a light shower of white dust. Cheryl sat and looked. One of the factory buildings across the tracks still had angles of glass in some of the windows, broken glass, of course, but angular shapes of the remains of the windows. They caught the light just so and reflected it back to where Cheryl was sitting; and it was beautiful, pure glints of light, rich and sweet.

Rita had always been a good girl—always. That was true. It was also true that at times, and even for weeks at a time, Rita had been a perfect little snot. Cheryl could remember moments when she thought she would scream if she heard one more whining loud cry for just one more cookie. Of course, that was true. But Rita was a child. She didn't know how to behave, how to be pleasant when she didn't feel pleasant, or how to be patient when she didn't get exactly what she wanted, not right away and not, in fact, ever. Cheryl reflected that plenty of adults didn't know how to be pleasant or patient or accepting. How could she expect a child to have mastered it? In time Rita grew to be a nice young woman, and that was fine. And the process had been fine. Holding her when she cried while she was teething, rocking her back and forth or carrying her from room to room, and Rita only drifting off to sleep when she was completely exhausted from crying—well, no, that wasn't fun but it was fine and Rita and Cheryl got through it. It was like that with most things. The bad parts they got through, and the good parts they relished. Together. It was always good.

It was when it was especially good, when Rita brought her a picture so laughingly inept and yet so perfectly what it was, so essential and clear in detail even if inexactly drawn, or when Rita was folded in her lap and Cheryl was reading to her and Cheryl paused in her reading, wondering if Rita had fallen asleep, and Rita immediately saying, "Don't stop, keep going" . . . when it was especially good Cheryl always felt the pull of sadness that she hadn't kept Laura. They would have been okay. The three of them would have been fine. At the time, with the two babies right there in front of her squalling and kicking and waving and all pink and red, Cheryl just didn't know what she could do. She didn't know how capable she was. She did what seemed best. But. Oh sigh.

You don't know how to live. You just live.

Rita always had friends; her friends came and went. It was usual for children. But when John Thomas came around, well, that was different. There had even been boys before, but this time it was different. John was not by any leap of fantasy a young man destined for great things, but he was a young man destined to take over his father's business, and that was enough. Dwayne Thomas had inherited Thomas Printing from his father, but he hadn't stood pat on just being the owner and operator of a printing concern, which was a good thing; printing was a challenging and changing business, and if he'd settled on merely that he'd probably be broke now. Dwayne had expanded into copying, which was a steady small income, but growing, and then expanded further into office supplies and then into office furniture. So Thomas Printing became Thomas Printing and Office Supplies, and it swelled up into different sections: the copying department and the furniture showroom and the office supplies retail area. They still did some printing, but as the building got larger, the printing aspect of things had been shunted way to the back beside the warehouse area that kept the retail departments stocked. When John Thomas appeared at Cheryl's door, looking for Rita, he was already in charge of the warehouse end of things; and there was no doubt that he, an only son, would eventually be running the whole business.

A good boy. A good young man. He carried himself quietly and with bright eyes looking around, observant of everything, which was a quality Cheryl appreciated even more than his probable financial soundness. Money could be found, but quality in a person was rare; appreciation for life was rare. Cheryl liked him just fine.

Rita was embarrassed but acquiescent to John's attention. They seemed a little stiff and formal with each other at first, but over time they relaxed into enjoying each other, sometimes in ways that were so silly Cheryl shuddered and made herself scarce. She never liked baby talk herself, not even in babies, and it sort of made her feel sick to hear adults engage in it. John would sit on the couch, and Rita would sit right next to him, gradually sliding right on top of him; and they would giggle and nuzzle and tickle and pretty soon slip into their goofy made-up language with each other, and Cheryl would find something to do somewhere beyond earshot. If it made them feel cozy with each other to talk like complete idiots, it was none of Cheryl's concern. Her place, she could see quite clearly, was to stay out of the way.

Late at night, lying in her bed, she would be awakened by rustles and sighs and the squeaking sound of the front-room couch being rhythmically bounced, punctuated by Rita making shushing noises. Cheryl knew that Rita was embarrassed, but there was no reason for shame. It was life. Right down to the squeaking rhythm of the couch, it was just the rhythm of life, and it was good. Cheryl would focus on not hearing and go back to sleep.

It was clear that John Thomas had something in his pants, something that wanted Rita bad, but what wasn't at all clear to Cheryl was whether or not John Thomas had anything in his head. Did the boy know anything, and did he think at all? Could the boy think at all? He did know the warehouse, and he could think clearly about it, apparently, and he would probably be able to run the business. Rita had brains to spare, so she would help him. But John Thomas seemed to Cheryl just as bland and blank as a white piece of paper. He shared with Cheryl the habit of looking around. He seemed to always be absorbing, always watching, but without judgment, simply being. That was attractive to Cheryl even though it didn't seem to be accompanied by a fierce, or even gentle, intelligence. And of course, he had that thing in his pants, and Rita appeared to enjoy it. Otherwise. Otherwise?

He tried to talk to Cheryl, but he could never seem to think of anything to say, and he would just blurt out facts. It was sort of comical but sort of sad too.

One night, her hands deep in dishwater and John lounging at the table while Rita was off puttering around somewhere, Cheryl said, "Come over here and dry these dishes, John, and we'll talk."

John sprang to his feet. "Well sure, Ms. McGovern—"

"Cheryl, John, you call me Cheryl."

"Yes, okay, yes . . . Cheryl." The boy—he was a man now, but Cheryl could only see a nervous little boy—snapped up a dish towel and started rubbing a coffee cup energetically as if trying to remove a stain.

"Just dry them, John. Don't hurt them."

"Yes . . . Cheryl," and he gingerly put the cup in the cupboard after looking around aimlessly and lost for a few minutes, struggling to remember where they went.

Cheryl smiled into her hot dishwater.

"Fifteen hundred reams of typing paper today! Ms. . . . Cheryl. We found space for it, that and the flats of cardboard boxes, but it was a chore." John nodded with assurance, looking down and selecting another coffee cup. "Yup, it was a chore."

Well, Rita liked him. That was the important thing.

Three days later Rita said she and John wanted to have coffee with Cheryl and talk about something. At that point, it was completely unnecessary. Cheryl knew exactly what they wanted to talk about, but she went along with the game. Rita was nervous even suggesting it, and Cheryl didn't want to make the poor girl suffer any more than she had to.

It was painful enough for everyone, but they got through it just fine. John Thomas and Rita were going to be married in four weeks. Pretty soon, pretty quick. Cheryl assumed that all that bouncing on the front-room couch had led to a bun in the oven, but she let that go unmentioned. She figured, correctly as it worked out, that Rita would tell her she was pregnant around a week or so after the wedding. Long enough to look more or less correct if you didn't look. So Cheryl would be a grandma, and that was good. That was something to celebrate and look forward to. What she didn't like at all was when John joshingly said in his awkward way, "So I guess now I'll call you mom." Cheryl stared at him hard and said hopefully clearly but not unkindly, "No. Cheryl, John, you call me Cheryl. I'm not your mom." The boy startled back from her as if she had slapped him but recovered quickly, nodding and saying, "Right. Right. Of course. Cheryl." At least they got that clear.

Without a thought, Cheryl lit another cigarette and stood up from her perch on the white concrete. The train was coming, a bit late maybe, but right on time according to its own time, which is all anyone can expect from anything. Cheryl gazed around uncritically at the trash trees, the ailanthus and mulberry, the weeds and shoots of weeds just dying off in the mixed gravel and dirt and dust and ash, at the steady bright tops of the rails reflecting the light of the lead locomotive; and finally she just stood and looked away, high into the depth of the clear blue sky, the forever of everything just as it was. The train was passing, but she was looking up into the air. Each car was passing, pulled without option by the car in front of it, dragging the car along behind it, the chain of effects from the cause of the locomotives, the steady drill of what happens, what happens next.

It had all moved rather quickly, and looking back it seemed easy and clear. Yes, John Thomas and Rita were married in a rather large wedding. John's father, Dwayne, was a local pillar of some sort, an active, engaged businessman; and for those types, a wedding appeared to be both a chance to cash in on and a chance to renew, or test, local connections. The wedding and reception were enormous, packed with people Cheryl and Rita had never seen and probably a lot of people John Thomas had never seen. Most of them got staggering drunk on the booze Dwayne provided. And they gave huge sums of money to the newlyweds to help them get started. In the old days, or perhaps in other social classes, people gave newlyweds toasters and comforters and dishes and all the various accoutrements of housekeeping. This seemed to be a cash-and-greeting-card sort of society, embossed large sentimental cards with huge checks inside them. It was plenty to get Rita and John Thomas started.

And then like boxcars following the engines, the boys came, the first well before Rita and John had been married nine months. No one even bothered to suggest that William, their fat healthy first boy, was premature. Barely a year later, Gerald was born; and Cheryl got to be the babysitting grandma she always wanted to be, rustling around her house with a baby on her hip and another crawling around on the floor, feeding and singing to and reading to and bouncing and laughing with her lovely, perfect grandchildren.

And then.

Cheryl sighed.

She had barely noticed but the train had passed. Usually she let herself go into the landscape, absorbed in just looking and being, letting everything in and letting everything out; usually she would have noted and then dismissed a thousand details of even such a short train, the bent rungs under a gondola, the almost art of the graffiti on this or that boxcar, the burned and dented sides of the cars, the sighing and squeaking and the smell of it all. But instead this one time she had been absorbed in her reverie and hardly noticed the train as it passed into the curve and vanished. Gone.

All of it gone. The violent blast of the wreck and then the funeral with one large coffin flanked by two small coffins and the useless words of the same pastor who had performed their wedding. And Rita in the hospital, then Rita back home.

Cheryl sighed without thinking, sighed deeply, and let all her thought out, spent it all. Without a brain in her head, she simply let her eyes turn slowly and take in the immediate landscape. Wreck and ruin. Burned and twisted metal. Shattered concrete. Ashes and dirt. Dying weeds and flourishing weed trees. Broken glass dangling from broken windows. The graffiti-marked walls, the sliding-away and collapsing roofs. Nothing. Dirt and dust and nothing. And over it all the wide empty blue sky like a meaningless statement or an unanswerable question.

4

Winston County Prosecutor Dan Danovitch had found his experience with Lance Thompson to be one of the most disturbing and unsettling experiences of his career, and that was saying quite a lot. He had administered, if not directly prosecuted, some of the weirdest and sickest crimes imaginable; and it had required him going into the events of these crimes in every sordid and lurid detail. He had seen more than enough of the ugliness of human life and death and interaction to keep him nervously awake for the rest of his life. That is, if he had been a delicate sort. He wasn't. Fifty-five, fit, with silver temples on his square handsome head, dressed head to foot in brown (what his daughter Mandy called his Smoky the Bear suit), he carried himself with alert confidence and a sort of air of being able to face and control any situation.

But Lance was different. To begin with, the case was strikingly violent in an unusual way. Lance Thompson, a moderately well-built fourteen-year-old, had confronted three boys older and much larger and stronger than him; and in a matter of seconds, he had beaten them to death. With his bare hands. He had attempted to reach a fourth boy who fortunately for everyone involved was smart enough to run away.

His initial examination of Lance had not gone well. Lance was seated quite still at a table in the interview room with his hands cuffed together in front of him, his face a complete blank. An armed guard stood in the corner just about in reach of Lance. Dan walked in briskly and snapped open his briefcase on the table, saying quickly, "Lance

Thompson, I'm Dan Danovitch, the county prosecutor, and I need to talk to you about your upcoming trial so we can figure out the best way for us to handle some issues. You're entitled to fairness, of course, and it's important that you're not even an adult. I'd like to go over some things with you and your attorney."

Dan sat, and Lance continued to sit, not moving or looking. Dan looked around but didn't see an attorney, only Lance and the guard. "Lance?"

Lance sighed lightly as if awaking from a nap, blinked, and said, "I'm not going to trial."

"You should have an attorney here with you."

"He's coming . . . soon."

Dan glanced at his watch. "Well then, we won't go over anything substantive until he gets here, but I think I can assure you that there will be some kind of trial."

Lance glanced at Dan. "Maybe so, maybe some sort of trial, but I won't be there."

"Oh? Are you planning to be out of town? Maybe going on a vacation?"

"I'm not going to stay in here, I'll tell you that."

"Hmm . . . I think we've got some bars and handcuffs and guards and guns and cameras and security systems that say different. I don't think you're going anywhere for a long time."

"We'll see."

"*I* know, Lance, I know. *You'll* see."

Lance's eyes lit up. "I know things. I know I won't be here for a trial, and I know all sorts of other things that there's no way I should know. I have ways of finding things out that I don't understand, that no one can understand, but I know things."

Dan stared at Lance, barely nodding.

"I see. You're some kind of psychic."

"I don't know about that. Things just come to me all at once, that's all. If that's psychic, then I guess I am. It's sort of a gift and sort of not a gift." Lance shrugged. "I just know things, that's all."

"Uh-huh." Dan frowned and started pushing papers around that he'd taken from his briefcase, his brown briefcase. He smiled thinking of Mandy and her teasing him for his Smoky the Bear outfit, the man in brown.

Lance was watching him carefully. "You frown. You smile. Are you unstable?"

Dan raised his eyebrows. "Well, I never killed anyone."

Lance made a dismissive gesture. "That just happened. It just happened. I didn't mean to kill anybody. I just hit them. Then they died. I know lots of things, but I don't know why they died."

Dan held up his hands. "Ah, you better hold that kind of talk until your lawyer gets here." Dan glanced at his watch again. "You do have a lawyer, don't you? And he is coming, isn't he?"

"I guess my dad hired somebody. Dad wanted to come, but they wouldn't let him."

"A good father, a bad son."

"Country and Western song?"

Dan smiled quickly, more as if in pain than as if amused. "Something like that."

Lance looked around the room and then back at Dan. "Well, if we can't talk about my alleged crime, let's talk about you. I'll tell you what I know about you. Let me think for a minute and see what rises to the surface."

"Please spare me. I'm not interested in your delusions of knowledge."

"You sexually abuse your wife," Lance said levelly as if it was a foregone fact.

"You aren't too old to spank, young man," Dan said, equally levelly.

Lance's brow wrinkled with a hint of perplexity. "I don't think you can do that, can you?"

"I wouldn't bother. I'm not your father. Thank god. Is this sex-abuse talk an example of your psychic ability?" Dan began sifting through his papers.

"Well, like I said, I know things, I get strong feelings about things, and they're always right in some sense. I don't know anything about sex, so maybe I'm wrong somewhere in what exactly is happening. It's just a feeling of you're having trouble in that department. Things aren't right somehow."

"Yes. Maybe you are 'wrong somewhere.'" Dan held a paper up as if he was reading it, but he was looking directly at Lance. "There's a note here that in one of your preliminary interviews, you told the interviewer that her husband was abusing her. Is this like a favorite topic of yours?"

Lance shrugged. "It's like I said. It's a feeling I get, that's all."

"Uh-huh. Turns out she wasn't even married. So you said it was her boyfriend. Turns out she didn't have a boyfriend either. I don't think I'll have you pick any horses for me."

"Well, look, there was something going on with Laura. She blushed, and she almost admitted sex was abusive for her."

"Almost admitted."

"Let me think." Lance scrunched his face and went into a rather exaggerated pose of someone thinking very hard, almost an imitation of thought.

Dan dramatically tapped his fingers on his papers, a display of fake patient waiting. Lance sat with his eyes closed. Suddenly his eyes snapped open.

"You and your wife don't have sex at all. That's it. She's a drunk. You can't stand her."

"That's enough."

"Now, you have a daughter Mandy—"

Dan was on his feet and leaning over the table. The guard stepped up immediately next to Lance and put his hand forcefully on Lance's shoulder. Dan's eyes drilled into Lance with total fury. "Shut up, boy. Shut up."

With that, he swept his papers into his briefcase, snapped it shut, turned, and walked out the door, trailing behind him: "I'll call your lawyer," and then to the guard, "Take him back to his cell."

That was just the beginning of the Lance case, but it turned out to be almost the last time Dan saw him. Still beside himself with anger at Lance mentioning his daughter, Dan immediately called the boy's lawyer, who turned out to be some kind of bumbling idiot. Mr.

Thompson might be a good father in most ways, but he wasn't helping his son much in the legal department. Attorney Sly Adams had confused the interview time, and the date, according to his mechanical-sounding and utterly disinterested secretary. It would have to be another day. Could we reschedule? Dan thought that was just fine. He rather liked the idea of Lance Thompson's problems entering a sort of limbo that would involve the boy staying in jail just as long as possible with no movement forward in his case at all. Dan liked that. Let the boy sit. Let the boy sit forever.

The next day Dan received a worn and dirty interoffice envelope with his name scrawled in the To box and the name Lance scrawled in the From box. Dan flipped open the envelope and pulled out two glossy 8" x 10" color photographs. The first was a picture of Dan lighting a Jack-O-lantern. His wife was sprawled in her easy chair beyond him fast asleep with her mouth hanging open. Drunk. The very night before Dan had carved the pumpkin by himself while his wife and Mandy were asleep. He had been irritated that the family had descended into such a mild enactment of what used to be a fun tradition for all of them. It had taken Dan repeated attempts to get the Jack-O-lantern lit, which was just more irritation on a generally unhappy evening. But this picture, the picture that apparently Lance had sent him, could only have been taken from inside the house, directly in the entryway beside the steps upstairs.

That was baffling and bothersome enough; but before he could think it through, he glanced on at the next picture, and that really set him off. It was a picture of Mandy, his thirteen-year-old daughter, fast asleep in her bed. The picture could only have been taken by someone standing directly beside the bed, only a few feet from Mandy. At that point, Dan lost control. First he felt like he was having a heart attack. Then he felt like he would vomit. Then he felt like he was going insane. He lurched around his office bellowing like a wounded cow, or so people told him later. He couldn't remember making a sound. He knocked over chairs, banged against a file cabinet, and finally got ahold of the telephone and called, almost shouting, for Lance Thompson to be brought immediately to Interview Room Number One.

Dan thundered down the steps to Interview Room Number One with visions of Lance Thompson and Dan's hands clenched tightly around his throat, strangling him. Or maybe Dan striking him, slapping him full in the face. Or at least, at the very least, shouting at him with no restraint at all. When he got there, the room was empty. Dan began pacing.

The phone rang, and a voice said that Lance Thompson was gone. He had been there this morning, but now he was gone. He had vanished.

Dan sat down at the table and began rocking slowly back and forth. Gradually he calmed down somewhat. The world wasn't red anymore. He was breathing smoothly. He pulled the pictures out of the envelope. There was a note he hadn't noticed before, clumsily written in ballpoint on a paper towel like the paper towels in the courthouse restrooms. Or the county jail, for that matter. It said, "Dan, you should find another line of work. It would be better for you and your family. Lance."

There was nothing Dan could do about it. He had daydreams of doing things about it, but the boy Lance had simply vanished. No one could figure out how he got away. There were no clues. Nothing to indicate how he made his way out of jail or where he might have gone. The pictures were equally mysterious. Dan would never know how they were taken or who took them. The whole deal made him by turns nervous and irritable and angry and, ultimately, afraid.

As days and then weeks went by without anything happening, Dan gradually relaxed about the whole affair. Apparently the boy wasn't going to do anything. What had seemed a threat when he first read it began to seem like someone's well-meant advice: "It would be better for you and your family." Looking at the picture of Mandy, Dan had thought the boy was saying he was going to hurt her if he didn't quit his job. But it didn't seem so. He didn't quit his job, and yet nothing happened. It seemed the boy really just meant that being a prosecuting attorney wasn't good for his family. There was no follow-up to the pictures. Lance broke out of jail, and then he disappeared. There had to be someone outside the jail helping Lance, but every search came up empty; there was some kind of conspiracy at root there, but no one could find anything. Case closed. Or rather, case filed away until something else happened. What puzzled Dan was why the pictures had been sent at all. If it wasn't a threat, what was the point?

Gradually Dan thought about it less and less. In time he came to a sort of a conclusion that all the boy wanted was to show off his magic powers, his psychic ability, which evidently went so far as to enable him to summon up pictures, actual photographs, of Dan's private life. Dan didn't believe for a minute that the boy was psychic, but he was certainly weird. And there was just no solution to the mystery of the pictures or Lance's escape. It was just one of those things. In fact, Dan couldn't think of anything in his life anywhere near as odd as this, so it wasn't "just one of those things." It was a unique thing, but over time he dismissed it. There was no solution, so he dismissed it and let it go. Experience suggested to him that eventually Lance would resurface, but Dan wasn't sure how far experience mattered in a case as unusual as this.

Dan's attitude toward people in general wasn't at all strange for people in law enforcement. According to this line of thought, there were basically three types of folks. First were the truly good people, and they were rare. Once in a while, you met someone who simply seemed incapable of a bad thought or a bad word or a bad action, the sort of people who thought of others first and barely thought of themselves at all, moving humbly and quietly through life making the best of each day and each interaction with others. A rare sort, but there were some of them out there. Dan had known a few.

Then there were the citizens, as Dan and many police personnel called them, and they were the common mass of people. The citizens were basically honest and basically good. They went through life without particularly wanting to hurt anyone else or make trouble for law enforcement. But things happen. A citizen could easily be in a car wreck, a citizen could be in an argument with a spouse or a neighbor that got out of hand, or a citizen could fudge a little on making tax payments or paying debts. There were many ways a citizen could slip up and slide outside the proper life, legally speaking. Citizens who made mistakes had to be arrested and had to be prosecuted, but basically Dan's job and the general job of the police was protecting citizens, not hunting them down or troubling them. A citizen who was caught breaking the law generally straightened right up and didn't break it again, not much. Breaking the law and getting in trouble with the police was something they wanted to avoid. A convicted citizen rarely did anything to get convicted again.

It always surprised and irritated Dan that many of the citizens didn't seem to believe that the third category of people actually existed. These were the bad guys. It was very simple. Those old cowboy movies had it right on this point. There were certain people, the guys in black hats, who were just plain bad. They were born bad, and they lived bad, and they died bad. The notion of reforming them into being citizens was just plain crazy talk. Most of Dan's job and most of the police's job was catching and convicting and putting away bad guys, putting them away where they wouldn't bother the citizens. There was no point in being sentimental about it; some people were just plain bad.

Even though Lance Thompson had beaten three young men to death with his bare hands, it was Dan's impulse to place the boy as a citizen. There was something quirky about all of it that didn't seem to place Lance in the bad-guy category. He had certainly fought like a professional and certainly killed those young men. But it didn't seem to Dan that Lance had set out to kill them. In a normal surge of adolescent self-righteousness and a misplaced sense of family honor, he had gone down to the high school parking lot to punish the four boys who had beat up his brother. The deaths were an almost accidental result from Lance's activities. In fact, as the details of the case developed, it seemed more likely to Dan that the boys Lance attacked were the bad guys. These boys made a normal practice of getting drunk and going out and beating people up. Often they would go out to lover's lanes, interrupt couples making love, humiliate them, and beat them. Those boys could very well have been bad guys. Not that they deserved to die, but . . .

As for Lance, and what he was, and what he was about, perhaps he would resurface at some point and Dan would know. Until then it was just a puzzle without a solution.

Two years later, Mandy Danovitch, now fifteen, disappeared. She simply disappeared. Dan was as agitated as any parent would be; his wife, Marie, completely collapsed into an unrestrained alcoholic stupor. Dan found himself at once frantic with worry about his daughter and yet distracted by the process of checking Marie into the hospital and getting her started on detox, confined and restrained in the arms of the health system. Marie was no help at all and actually a further complication and burden. What would happen to Marie was something that through years of her alcoholism Dan had learned to not look at, not think about. But now in this crisis of Mandy being lost, he suddenly had to confront Marie's desperate addiction, the thing Dan had always minimized as being her problem, Marie's problem.

Mandy's disappearance made no sense. No one knew anything. Her friends all denied that Mandy had ever said anything about running away, and there was no clue that Mandy had been planning to disappear. She was just gone for no reason.

Dan assumed she had been grabbed by someone, and he had a pretty good professional sense of how these kinds of cases usually turned out. He tried not to think about it. He tried to set aside his clear knowledge of what sort of road he and Marie were probably on. He was hugely relieved when after two days of nothing he suddenly got a call from an unknown obviously disguised voice that Mandy had been kidnapped and her ransom was $1 million and someone would be in touch about the details. So now Mandy's disappearance was not a weird sex crime perpetrated by some insane and totally unpredictable pervert but rather a business proposition by someone, probably some group of people, out for mere cash. A predictable rational sort who could be dealt with.

Of course the caller warned him not to involve any law enforcement types, but that was just a gesture. You can't kidnap the county prosecutor's daughter and seriously expect law enforcement types not to be involved instantly; Dan was a law enforcement type himself. Once a ransom had been asked for, he didn't hesitate to call in the FBI and encourage them to set up a unit right in his office, tapping his phones and setting up computers that the agents or assistant agents or whatever they were gazed at continuously for no particular reason Dan could discern. He guessed it had something to do with Mandy, but he couldn't imagine what it might be other than trolling through records looking for a match for this essentially unexceptional case. It was a simple kidnapping, a demand for money Dan certainly didn't have but could probably get with federal assistance. It probably looked like any of a couple of dozen other kidnapping cases.

Dan went through the motions of continuing to do his work in his now-overcrowded office. Not knowing what else to do, he started sorting through his inbox and found an interoffice memo envelope with his name jotted in the To box and the name Lance written in the From box. Inside he found a letter:

I told you to find another job. I know Mandy has disappeared, and I know she's been kidnapped. I didn't have anything to do with it, and I'm looking into it for you just to show it wasn't me. You need to stall them as long as you can. You convicted a mule two months ago, and his boss in Chicago wanted revenge, so he ordered Mandy killed. The locals who took her decided on their own to make some money out of the job, but they have no intention of letting her go. They're going to kill her. So you have to stall. I'm pretty sure I can get her back to you, but you have to stall.

That was it. The FBI agents weren't impressed. They started looking into the boss in Chicago in a vague way; but they didn't think that Lance, a sixteen-year-old boy, actually knew anything or could do anything. Dan agreed with them, but he couldn't help but hope. The boy was unusual. There was no doubt about that. Maybe. Maybe? Mostly the note just added another layer of complexity and agitation to the whole situation. But Dan had to hope. Otherwise, stalling was part of the plan anyway, so there wasn't anything to do in response to Lance's note except to be curious about it.

Two days later Mandy Danovitch called her father from the police station in Henderson, the county seat of the county just north of Dan's district. She was okay. She wanted to come home. She had been grabbed by four men from a plain white van as she was walking over to her friend's house. They gagged her, bound her with duct tape, and covered her head with a pillowcase. They told her to be quiet and behave herself. Of course, she was terrified, and she hardly struggled at all. After a brief ride in the country, or so she assumed since they didn't stop for many lights, she was guided into a house and down some stairs to the room where they had kept her for the last few days. Her leg was shackled to a chain that fit into a hook in a huge wooden beam that must have held up the whole house. She could reach a narrow bed with a sheet and blanket, and she could reach an open toilet. A television set was placed just beyond her reach, but they gave her a remote control. She guessed that one of the men must have a teenage daughter because he gave her a variety of nail polishes. So she watched TV, did her nails, and waited. They assured her that they had no intention of hurting her. They only wanted money, and when they got the money, she would be released all safe and sound. Three times a day they brought her TV dinners, which she didn't like at all; but by the second day, she was eating all of them and even, somewhat courageously, complaining that she wanted more to eat. And better food. The men just laughed at her. Other than bringing her meals to her, the men had nothing to do with her. She could hear men talking and walking around upstairs, but she could never hear anything clearly. She watched TV and did her nails again and again. And she waited.

She was asleep when the boy Lance opened the door and stepped in, leaving the door open behind him. He had a gun in his hand, a pistol with an unusually long barrel. He glanced around the room as he stuck the pistol in his belt and then walked up to her, smiling. "I'm going to get you out of here," he said, and he set to working on the shackle on her leg. There was nothing exceptional about him; he was just a boy about her age in a plain white T-shirt and jeans. He seemed a little unwashed.

"You're Mandy Danovitch, right?"

She nodded and watched his fingers working over her shackle. He seemed to know what he was doing, but she didn't see how he was going to get it loose. He didn't have any sort of tool or anything. He was just handling the lock gently and then with some force and then gently again.

"I'm Lance. I'm an acquaintance of your father's. Just do what I say, and we'll get you out of here."

Mandy was a little tired of men telling her to behave and do what they said, but Lance was obviously different. All at once, he had the lock loose, and Mandy was rubbing her ankle and feeling hugely relieved. Lance took the pillowcase off her pillow.

"Now, Mandy, there's some stuff upstairs I don't want you to see, so I'm going to put this over your head and hold your hand and lead you out. We'll go quickly, and as soon as we get in the van and get down the road, you can take the pillowcase off. But just leave it on and hold my hand and come with me. There's some stuff you shouldn't see."

So her eyes covered, she took his hand and followed him up the stairs, stumbling a little once or twice. Then the door and they were out on the porch, and they were moving quickly now in a straight line. "Wait a minute," Lance said as he dropped her hand, and she heard a car door open right in front of her. Lance helped her up into the high seat of a van, and he shut the door carefully. In a moment, he was in the driver's seat, and they were driving away.

"You can take your hat off now."

Mandy pulled the pillowcase off and looked around. It was some seedy little town she had never been in, or so she thought until she saw the courthouse and recognized that it was Henderson. She looked down and noticed blood on her feet. Lance gave her the pillowcase and said, "Wipe your feet off with that." She did the best she could.

"Now, Mandy, listen." Lance handed her a piece of paper. "There's an address on there where they held you. There's also the address of a pool-hall bar-type place. Tell your dad they need to check those two places." Lance looked at Mandy as if waiting for an answer, so she said, "Okay." Then he went on, saying, "Now tell your dad that I'm going up to Chicago and he doesn't need to worry about that guy anymore. And tell your dad he should get into a new line of work."

With that, he dropped her at the police station across from the courthouse and drove off.

Wesley Meredith, the chief of police in Henderson, called to give Dan a report.

"Mandy okay?"

"Yeah, she's fine. She's seems to think now it was just an adventure, though she does admit she was completely terrified the whole time and felt sick. She might have some kind of crush on the boy who saved her. I guess I can understand that. What do you know?"

"How's Marie?" Everyone everywhere seemed to know what a wreck Dan's wife was.

"She's . . . delighted. She was so happy to get Mandy back. They just held each other and cried and cried. Maybe things will be different now. I don't know."

"Good, good, that sounds great, Dan."

"So what do you know?"

"Well, right. We checked out the house where Mandy was held. A dead guy in the bushes out front with a bullet hole in the middle of his forehead. Then in back, next to the back porch, a dead guy with a bullet hole in his left temple. The boy must have been using a silencer or something. He knocked them off without bothering anybody. So. Then in the kitchen two guys dead, each with a bullet hole in the head, one in the forehead and one in the temple. So. Four shots and four dead men. *Boom. Boom.* Very efficient."

"Jesus. Who were they?"

"Oh, um, two of them worked for Bill Peterson, a local drug pusher and pimp and general all-purpose criminal who ran Bill's Pool Hole. We never quite caught him. But he was into everything: stolen property, drugs, sex, gambling."

"Okay."

"So two of these guys worked for him, on the staff of the Pool Hole so to speak, and then the other two were known associates. Punks."

"Okay. So the other address must have been Peterson's place. You checked that?"

"Yeah. It was a slaughter, Dan, an absolute slaughter. It looked like they were playing cards, Peterson and three men and two women, all either employees of the Hole or known associates. All of them dead, each with one bullet to the head. A bloodbath. He must have just walked in and started blasting, though with perfect accuracy: six bullets and six dead people."

"My my. My my my."

"Who is this kid, this Lance fellow?"

"I don't know, Wes. I really don't know."

"Can we find him?"

"I don't think so. He told Mandy he was going to Chicago to take care of someone. We've been looking for him for a couple of years without seeing the least sign. He's, um, impossible."

"I wouldn't want to be whoever he's looking for in Chicago. Quite the psychopath I guess, a real killer. He sure cleaned Henderson up."

"I don't know, Wes. I just don't know."

5

It was an absurd apartment really, but as Rita cheerfully observed, they were an absurd couple. All the apartments in the Crestview Apartments were identical, though some were mirror images of the others. You went in the front door, and to one side there was a bathroom and then a bedroom. Directly ahead and stretching to the other side was the general living area, an expanse at once the dining room and living room with a kitchen lining the door-side wall, a refrigerator and then sink and kitchen cabinets including the luxury of an actual dishwasher. Neither Rita or Laura had ever had one of those, and they were sort of afraid of it. The wall across from the kitchen wall was entirely glass, huge wide windows that let in endless light.

What Laura and Rita rented was the suite. It was the only apartment of its kind in the building. The central dividing wall had been removed from two apartments on the top floor of the Crestview, looking out on the wooded hill behind the building. So Rita and Laura had two of everything in a mirror reversal, which meant two outside doors and two kitchens with two dishwashers to be afraid of; but it also meant an enormous living area for an apartment, with vast pleasant windows. They each had their own bedroom and bathroom at the far ends of the living area. It was perfect for them. It was also absurd.

It was slightly more expensive than they wanted, but it seemed to fit them so perfectly they snatched it up. Both of them working as waitresses certainly wouldn't make living easy, but when you got down to it, they could share everything far more easily than most couples.

They were after all mostly identical. And they never ever crowded each other. Being together, living together, was as natural and easy as being alone but with better company.

Laura immediately hung birdfeeders outside the windows, hoping she would attract all sorts of birds from the wooded hills that surrounded the Crestview. Unfortunately, she didn't get much. A few brown sparrows and some house finches like blushing red sparrows would pick at the food some days but otherwise not much.

"I don't understand. I put out premium cardinal food," she complained to Rita.

Rita responded, "Maybe this neighborhood doesn't have premium cardinals," and they laughed and let it go. If it got cold enough, if there was enough snow in the winter, they would probably get all the birds Laura wanted.

What Rita wanted was a cat. A big fat cat that would saunter through the apartment once or twice a day and then the rest of the time sleep in a sunbeam, moving only to follow the sunbeam.

"I like birds," Laura said, almost scolding, "and you want a cat. Are you my twin or some kind of evil anti-Laura?"

"Some twisted design underlies everything," Rita said heavily, but she was smiling.

"What's that? What's that?" Laura grinned hugely. "Where did you get that?"

Rita struck an airy superior pose. "I have my sources of wisdom. I'm not as foolish and ignorant as you might think I am."

"Oh, come on, you're at least as foolish and ignorant as I think you are."

They immediately stuck out their tongues at each other and then laughed.

"Well, it's from a soap opera."

"A soap opera?" Laura waved around the apartment. "On which TV we don't have were you watching a soap opera?"

Rita pointed directly to a spot beside the door, her door. "That one!" Of course, there was nothing there. They both laughed and touched, hands touching. Then Rita slouched back at the kitchen table and took a pull at her cup of coffee.

"It is from a soap opera. I was looking through the paper, and I ran across these little one paragraph summaries they have, on Saturdays I guess, of each soap opera's plot so far. They're ridiculous. I love them. Mostly it's just 'Betty knows she's pregnant, but she doesn't know if it's Jim or Bob, and meanwhile Bob has proposed to Julie Ann and Jim has cancer.'" They both laughed. "But one of them suddenly said, 'Some twisted design underlies everything,' and I thought, 'My god, are we in an Anne Tyler novel?'"

"Hmm. I was thinking bad philosophy, but maybe you're right, one of those thoughtful novels about average people like you and me."

"Right. Average. With premium cardinals feasting at our feeders, how can we be average?"

"Now, Rita"—Laura chuckled—"we only put out premium cardinal food. We haven't actually seen any of them on the wing. Perching. Eating. Anything!"

"Well, 'all things excellent are as difficult as they are rare.'"

Laura raised her eyebrows. "Dear me. Spinoza. I do believe I underestimate you."

"I do believe you do," Rita said almost seriously, but then she added as if in song, "Do-do-do-do."

Neither of them had done a touch of waitressing since they were in high school, but as with the apartment, they knew without saying anything that they were only going to take particular kinds of jobs, jobs that would suit them. That essentially meant that they would be working together, that they would be able to see and talk to each other, or at least glance at each other and make their facial signals back and forth. Now that they had found each other, they weren't one bit interested in letting the world get between them again. As long as they were both working, they could get by on about any old money at all, and at this point all they wanted to was to get by—to get by together. All their ambitions were centered on each other or, rather, on the unit, the single one, they formed by being together.

Marge confessed that she only needed one waitress and glanced at Rita, the handicapped one, as if saying clearly but silently, "I don't need this one." Laura immediately spoke up, "Well, that's fine. We understand. Thank you for considering us and giving us your time." She turned to go, tugging mildly at Rita's elbow.

"Hold on, hold on," Marge called out in a good-humored sound as if she was dismissing what she had said as mere thinking mistakenly out loud. "I don't *need* two waitresses right now, but I could use two waitresses I guess until you girls build up your clientele. This is mostly a lunch joint, but we're trying to get the breakfast deal off the ground, and it's slow going. If I think about it, I could probably handle all the breakfast business myself as it is now. But two lovely girls like you sashaying around, making friendly with the farmers—what farmers?— anyway, guys going into town for work each morning, well, I could try it out and see. The two of you might be just what we need to get this thing rolling."

Marge wasn't exactly a financial wizard, and she didn't at all want to be a financial wizard; she just wanted to keep the place going and build up a day-long business. As long as the building was standing there all day, they may as well try to have paying customers in it all day. But whether or not hiring both women was a good financial decision was really beside the point. The twins intrigued her. They piqued her curiosity. Twins were neither here nor there with Marge. She'd seen all sorts of weird manifestations in nature that were considerably stranger than identical twins. These girls were nice and attractive, even the wounded one, and they seemed competent and bright. Marge couldn't quite zero in on the precise point, but something about the one being a damaged near copy of the other instead of an exact copy drew her attention and made her thoughtful, made her want to look and watch, to see them together. Maybe customers would feel the same way, but at the end of the day Marge didn't give a hang about the customers, not really. She wanted customers, but she wouldn't be beholden to them. She would even say sometimes loudly so everyone there eating could hear, "You know how they say 'The customer is always right'? Well, not in here, damn it." And everyone, mostly, would laugh, except perhaps the jerks she was aiming at. She wasn't kidding. Some customers were just not worth serving.

The more she thought about it, the more she wanted both of the girls. Just as they were, they were perfect. They seemed to fit with each other even better than twins who were identical would. And the longer they worked for Marge, the happier she was to have them, to have them both. At first they sort of entertained her, but as time went on, it seemed to Marge that she was learning something from them, though not anything she could put into words. It was something about all of life, something she could know but not say.

It was a thing to chew on more than one would think at first. Like anyone, Marge supposed, her first thought had been that it was so nice of Laura to be taking care of poor Rita. Obviously Laura was lighter on her feet than Rita, and she was more agile at chores like loading the dishes on the rack of the huge silver dishwashing complex that was one of the Spotlite's most expensive and impressive pieces of equipment; or putting fresh coffee on in another impressive piece of Spotlite equipment, the giant silver coffeemaker something like a huge plumber's nightmare of a bright samovar; or just setting out the silverware folded tight in single paper napkins. But really there wasn't much to pick from there. Laura looked quicker and smoother, but she wasn't really much quicker. Rita could and did work, and she kept up with her sister when she wanted to. But Rita paused to think more. She could hurry, but she never rushed. More and more, it seemed to Marge, that Laura was hustling around doing the easy stuff so Rita could focus on what was important. It was almost as if Laura was the assisting nurse and Rita was the gifted famous surgeon, the one who really knew what was going on, what needed to be done, and exactly how it needed to be done. Rita had the knowledge; Rita knew.

Laura had been nervous about getting jobs. Their needs were peculiar, and it seemed so unlikely that they would find something that would fit them both. Rita was quietly assuring that they would find something perfect. As it turned out, being waitresses at the Spotlite was perfect, or would have been perfect if it had paid twice as much. Most of their pay came from tips, and the tips were generous. Folks seemed to like Laura and Rita, but there just weren't enough of them. Marge was sure the business would grow, and their pay with it, but nothing much seemed to be growing at the Spotlite. It just waddled along. More money, mostly for more security, would have been nice, but . . . it was enough. They were making enough. They didn't need all that much.

The weeks slid by, and the layers of Laura and Rita being Laura and Rita together revealed themselves slowly and only by slight degrees. It took time to see what was right in front of them, all the ways they matched or overlapped or compensated for each other. And in time, they would see the parts that were still missing, though that would be an especially slow revelation.

Cheryl McGovern sat out in her folding wooden slat chair at the edge of the garden watching the day fade away. She often sat out if the evenings were fine, watching the twilight change of light in the cooling of the day; and sometimes she sat out in the morning, if she happened to be up, and watched the day drift in. It had occurred to her more than once that most people probably didn't have a garden chair. "Most people." The phrase always gave her a sour taste in her mouth. For her there was almost a tyranny loose across the land that was called "most people" and demanded absolute obedience. Her daughter Rita had been somewhat of a spear carrier and flag waver for the movement at a certain period of her early adolescence, but thankfully she outgrew it without too much scolding or cajoling from Cheryl. That was understandable; at the time, Rita was just a young girl, and she was still figuring out what mattered and what didn't. Of course, she was as self-absorbed as any early teen and worried over much about her image among her peers.

What Cheryl could never figure out is why grown-ups cared so much about what most people did, why an adult would assess herself in terms of what most people were doing and consider herself a failure if she didn't fit the bill of most people's wants and needs and actions. Or even thoughts—wanting to think what most people thought. Weird. As far as Cheryl could tell, most people didn't know the first thing about life, about how to live a full and genuine life. They were like clueless rats running around in a box trying to get what the other rats had, dropping whatever glittering object they were holding so they could snatch away some other rat's glittering object. Everything was all the same, or it was all different, but grasping and taking were irrelevant to being. It seemed irresistible that wanting to have what most people had led to wanting to have slightly more than most people had. As if just to be sure you were keeping up, it was best to get a little bit ahead. You were certainly blameless according to the measure of most people if you were superior to most people. The whole thing swelled out eventually into an explosion of impossible to satisfy desires meeting the empty nothingness of things, the lifelessness of things. Death—really, death, which didn't much matter either, if you looked at it right.

Cheryl liked to look, to see. She had had the same old wooden chair, her garden chair, forever, it seemed, though she knew that that was an exaggeration. She couldn't remember. It could be as long as twenty years that she had been carrying that same old chair out of her garage in the spring and setting it beside the garden and then lugging it back into the garage in the late fall. It stood all late spring and all summer and into the fall just there, at the end of the squash and gourds, rattled by rain and wind and sun and temperature change, the sweltering humidity of the Midwest; and it had held up fine for however long. Eventually she would replace it, she supposed; maybe the day after she set her butt down on it and her butt went right through it. Otherwise, it was a fine chair, and there was no need to replace it or ever spruce it up with a little paint. It was fine.

At some point, Rita told her, "Mom, you look just like Buddha sitting out there," and Cheryl unreflectively took it as a compliment. Buddha. As the years passed and her bulk slowly expanded and her movement slowed, she could even feel her mind slowing. She felt like she might be gradually becoming a sort of Buddha figure, sitting square and straight in her chair, completely still, looking without judgment, and often enough without even a thought, at the changing world in front of her. Yes. That was all. Cheryl liked to look, and that was a kind of general nonspecific yes to all of it. Maybe she was some sort of Buddha figure.

Cheryl had been poking around in the squash and gourds when she suddenly felt that she was done and it was time to let the day go. The squash were nice. They were good to eat, and they did well in her garden. It was the gourds, though, that really took off; whatever it was in Cheryl's ground or in the sky or the weather, it was perfect for gourds. They sent shoots out in every direction, and without Cheryl's firm hands at her hoe, they would have taken over the entire garden. More than a few times, Cheryl reflected that her garden wasn't of the right time. There were periods in human society when gourds were, if not precious, at least valuable items, things that could be used by everyone, holding water and serving as bowls or containers of whatever sort a person could imagine. But now? Now they just grew and grew, and Cheryl picked them and lined them up along her front porch edge; and there they sat like little Buddhas: fine enough to look at but no use at all to anyone as implements and certainly not good to eat.

She let herself down slowly into the slat wood chair, and she began to sit. Eyes wide, she gazed along the garden edge out toward the three-wire fence at her property end, though really she thought all of it—everything—belonged to whoever took the time to look, to really look at it and take it in. In a sense, whatever she studied carefully belonged to her forever. Past the fence, there was a blank flat field that had been hay earlier but had been cut utterly clean and now in the disappearing light looked almost like a wide field of gray concrete, gradually darkening to soft blue and then black. Farther on, silent from this distance, the woodlot stood with still leaves, crinkly and dry, some of them, the maples, gorgeous red and gold in the direct sun, but the oaks, which most of them were, more like trees dangling small paper bags, lunch bags, plain brown to soft red that would hang on almost through all of winter depending on the weather. The colors were falling away as the light seeped out of her field of vision. Oaks and maples together were sliding toward a level brown to gray.

In fact, as she widened her vision, everything was leveling in the failing light; and Cheryl let her eyes go, taking it all in equally without discrimination; and the far trees and the nearer gray field and the three-wire fence and the flourishing edge of her garden were all becoming the one thing of everything accepted together, a falling in and lining up and melting into one. And Cheryl let her mind go. She didn't judge or measure or think to name this or that; all of it was everything, and it was all rich and strange and beautiful.

Suddenly a white T-shirt appeared as if from nowhere. It was off beside a line of brush that marked the end of the cut hay field, a floating white T-shirt exactly the shape of its name. Cheryl's mind slipped back into focus, into analysis; and she guessed at once that the figure in the shirt had been hidden in the brush but as the evening came on felt courageous enough, safe enough, to step out into the clear field. Focusing her eyes in the dim light, and thinking carefully about what exactly she could see, she decided it was a boy, a teenage boy, standing and looking toward her or toward the house behind. It was the boy Lance. He wanted Laura. Laura wasn't here, of course, but he must have known Cheryl was and that Cheryl was Laura's mother. So. Cheryl sat very still. Then she quit focusing and let her eyes and then her mind right behind her eyes float back to the general, the broad scene, and the wide unity of everything. Only for a moment as her mind extinguished and the world went completely dark and the boy vanished from her sight she let herself have one clear thought: so it all moves on, and a different challenge begins.

6

Happy Wilson sat very still on a bench in Lincoln Park, a couple of blocks from his apartment. It wasn't a place he went to much, but he didn't want to sit inside and think. He was just too agitated by his day, seeing that boy. So he walked and thought, and then he sat and thought, easing himself down slowly onto one of the empty benches along the path. He sat somewhat leaning forward, wearing his tan trench coat, one of his few concessions toward the traditional picture of a private detective. Maybe he looked like a private detective or at least looked like people's idea of a private detective; he wasn't sure. He didn't really care. The park had fallen into darkness over an hour ago, and with the late-October night, it was getting cold; but Happy didn't feel it much. He was too busy thinking. The park was supposed to be dangerous after dark, but Happy didn't feel any danger. It was a cool night, and the park seemed completely empty except for him. He glanced around. The paved path curved up from the playground and passed by his feet and went on into the fall trees, maples throwing off their leaves. He hunched. He thought.

The boy Lance was a mystery. Nothing about him made much sense. Why was he looking for Laura? Why could he find Happy, whom he was sure knew where Laura was, but he couldn't seem to find Laura himself? Why was a sixteen-year-old boy wandering around like that at loose ends? How did he live? What was he up to?

It was clear enough to Happy that he had no interest at all in connecting Lance to Laura. In the morning, he would go back to boiling an egg himself in his own kitchen. The boy could be anywhere, and he might follow him. At this Happy glanced around, reassuring himself that the park was empty. He might follow him and find Laura regardless of Happy's clear decision not to tell him where she was. In time, if the boy didn't reappear, maybe Happy could start going back to the Spotlite; for now he would stay away. What would he do if the boy reappeared, if he showed up at his office again? Maybe he should call the police right now and get a report in on him. There was no sense in Happy trying to deal with a dangerous criminal, if that's what Lance was, or even in trying to deal with a rather demented juvenile delinquent, which seemed to be a more likely and accurate description of Lance.

"Hey, man, you want a blowjob?"

Happy jerked up and stared wild-eyed at the girl who had flopped down next to him.

"Whoa, whoa, cowboy, steady there!" She raised both her tiny hands as if gesturing a horse to be still. "Did you think you were all alone in the world?"

Happy looked up and down the park path; it was deserted, empty, and black except for the evenly spaced lights circled by wildly flying insects, maybe the last bugs of fall. He looked at the girl who was smiling vaguely. She looked like she might have weighed all of ninety-two pounds and as if she might be fifteen, though a very slight fifteen. Her hair was an off-blonde brown, cut short in a sort of tomboy cut, and Happy thought it must be the oiliest hair he had ever seen. Her skin wasn't too good, freckles barely winning in a competition with raw red acne. She was wearing a plain gray hoodie and worn-out jeans with gaping holes in them and sneakers that had once been pink, without socks.

"Do I want a blowjob?"

"Nah, nah, man," she said, shaking her head vigorously, "you misunderstood me. What I said was 'Do you want a blowjob?'"

Sarcasm—Happy understood that. He nodded and muttered, "Okay."

"Yeah?" She smiled and opened her eyes wide.

"No, no . . . I mean, I understand . . . but no, I don't want that at all, no, not at all."

She shivered a little and scrunched her shoulders. "Well, shit."

Happy gazed at her for almost a full minute. She looked like she had never eaten anything. She looked starved. "But we could make a deal."

She just looked at him. "Yeah?"

"How much does . . . what you said . . . cost?"

"You want to bargain?"

"No, just . . . how much would it cost if I said yes?"

"Fifty dollars."

"Okay." Happy nodded. "You talk to me, and I'll pay you $50. How's that?"

She gave him a sly grin. "You want me to talk dirty to you, daddy?"

Happy winced. "No . . . don't . . . don't call me that. I'm Happy."

She immediately burst into a deep raucous laugh, the first sign of genuineness she had shown. "Ah, you're happy. Okay then, no wonder you don't want a blowjob. You're already happy!" More laughter. Uncharacteristically but silently, Happy cursed, thinking, *My goddamn name, I hate my goddamn name.* He'd been through this sort of thing before, though not exactly.

The girl slapped her thighs, which were as thin as arms. "Maybe you'd like a blowjob just to celebrate being happy!"

Almost gritting his teeth, Happy said, "It's my name. My name is Happy."

The girl stopped laughing as if he had snapped a switch. "Okay, okay, so your name is Happy. Your parents must have been something."

They sat quietly, though she all at once chuckled a little and said softly, "Happy."

"Well then, my name is Cerise." She paused. "That means *red.*"

"Yes." Happy nodded as if nodding to himself and then paused. Slowly he said, "But what does *red* mean?"

Cerise chuckled and waved away vaguely, saying, "You're a real character, Happy, a real character. I think maybe I actually like you."

They sat and said nothing, staring straight ahead into the darkness.

"Okay, then, Happy, how long do I have to talk for $50?"

"A week."

That cracked her up again; and she doubled over, laughing her rich deep laugh, such a tremendous laugh for a girl so small.

"Stop, man, stop! You're killing me here!"

She wiped her eyes with her hands.

"Really now. You don't want dirty talk. You just want to talk. How long? I got work to do, you know."

"Well . . . Cerise"—and Happy shrugged and pushed out his hands—"that depends on the quality of your talk. If you talk good, if you can talk and tell me what I want to know, then this can be over quick, maybe in just a few words."

"Okay. Shoot. What do you want to know?"

Happy turned on the bench and looked directly at her, straight into her eyes, and she looked directly back at him with her large brown eyes as if to say "No foolin' now . . . what?"

"Okay, Cerise. What's it all about? What does it all mean? Why are we here, and what are we meant to do? What's it all about?"

"That's what you want to know?"

"Yes. Why are we here?"

"I'm here to suck cock."

Happy gave an exasperated grunt, waving his hands around quickly. "No, no, that's not what I mean. I don't mean 'Why are we in the park in the middle of the night?' I mean why are we anywhere, anywhere at all?"

"I'm here to suck cock."

"Cerise, that can't be it. We can't all be here, all the stars and the galaxies and whatever, everything, rivers and trees and people, and God knows what all just for that."

"I don't know anything about all that, Happy. I was just talking about me."

Happy sat back. Neither of them moved or said anything. The bugs circled the lights. The trees stood perfectly still, vague at the limits of the soft illumination. Happy and Cerise sat quietly.

"Okay. So."

The girl didn't move, and Happy paused for perhaps a full minute.

"Do you think we're all here for different reasons? Do you think it all means something different for each of us?"

"Well, of course."

Cerise shook her head and looked down, and her slight right hand reached out and gently touched Happy's leg. He held it still as if he expected a snake bite; but she only laid her hand on his leg for a moment, a gentle touch, and then she pulled back.

"Happy, you can't afford me. You shouldn't be out here. Take your money and go home and go to bed."

"I don't know . . . Cerise. This isn't really satisfactory."

"Well, I've told you all I know, and I've told you all I can do. I have to work now."

Happy looked up and down the park path; it was still utterly black except for the five or so lights they could see from their bench, slight flashes of light circling, the last insects. There was no one anywhere.

"I don't have $50," Happy said, reaching for his wallet, "but let me give you something so you can eat at least."

"No, Happy, I don't want your two bucks or whatever."

"Cerise . . . are you a drug addict?"

"What do you think, Happy? What do you think?" Her eyes flared out, and she spoke somewhat harshly, somewhat louder. She was almost angry.

Happy opened his hands in a gesture of ignorance.

"Do you think I *like* sucking strangers' dicks, Happy? Do you think I do it for *fun*? Or even *money*? Of course I'm an addict."

Happy quickly looked up and down the path again. On the next bench, maybe ten yards away, a young boy had suddenly materialized as if conjured out of the black night itself, a piece of white T-shirt and blue jeans with a boy inside miraculously built of nothingness and dark. It was Lance.

"What about him, Cerise? Is he a prospective client for you?"

Cerise leaned forward and looked around Happy at the boy on the bench. Immediately she sat back, sighed, and said, "No, he's nothing, nothing at all. He might beat me up and take my money, but he hasn't had fifty bucks of his own for a long, long time. He's a loser."

"You know him?"

"No, Happy, I just know the type. I know the type."

Happy spoke quickly to Cerise, "Help me. Help me. Say your name is Laura, okay? You're Laura."

"What?"

Happy was standing up and waving his arm.

"Lance!" he called. "Lance! You were right! I found her! I found Laura!"

Lance stood up, stared at Happy and Cerise for a moment, and then ran off up the path, ran away.

Happy lunged forward a couple of steps, shouting, "Lance! Lance! I've got her for you!"

The boy was gone.

And when Happy turned back, Cerise was gone too. Happy was alone in the dark.

At three in the morning, a furious pounding at his front door woke Happy up from his blank deep sleep. He struggled to the door without thinking and pulled it open, saying, "What? What?" Immediately a compact hard man pushed the door open and pushed himself into Happy's small apartment. Happy stepped back dazed, fumbling around for the lamp. The man shut the door, smoothly and carefully.

"What is it? What do you want?"

"My girl says you didn't pay her." The voice was calm but hard.

"Pay her? Pay who? Cerise?"

Happy had a lamp on now, and he looked at the man, head to foot. Whoever he was, he was hard and direct and fired up, flexing his muscles and clenching and unclenching his fists, bouncing a little on his feet. Happy stepped back, and the man stepped forward, keeping close.

"We just talked. We didn't do anything. We just talked."

The man stared at Happy as if Happy hadn't said anything at all.

"How did you get here? How did you find my apartment?"

"I was watching you the whole time, buddy," the man spit out quietly. "I followed you. I know you exactly. I know everything. And

I want the $50 you owe my girl, and I want another hundred for my trouble. Right now."

Happy stretched his hands wide. "I don't have that kind of money on me. I've got maybe $7. I can give you that. And I can meet you in the park and give you the $50 tomorrow. That's okay. That's fine. I'll do that, but that's all you'll get from me. We didn't do anything. We just talked."

Suddenly the man stood absolutely still, not flexing or clenching or bouncing.

Happy waited.

And then the man said, "Well, we have a problem."

And that was the beginning of the worst experience of Happy's life.

"Do you feel as bad as you look?"

Happy was lying very still in a hospital bed, maybe swathed from head to foot in bandages or a cast, an entire body cast. He couldn't tell. He couldn't see. In the front of his brain, there was a solid black onion shape, heavy and dark and slowly pulsing. Or maybe a turnip. Something. A heavy black something in the front of his brain. He couldn't see, but he could almost see this shape. He could feel it.

And he could hear the boy. He had tried to make it as clear as he could to the nurses and doctors that he didn't want any visitors, but somehow the boy Lance had gotten in anyway. He'd slid a chair right up next to Happy's bed, and he leaned toward Happy, perched over the bed rail. His voice was clear and close and irritating, and Happy hated it.

"That guy really made a mess of you."

"Gob abway."

"He was Candy's pimp, of course."

"I'b don'b care. Gob abway. Leeb be aloned."

"I don't know what you thought you were doing with Candy. Cruising for whores in the park? You're not like that. And then to tell me she was Laura. What were you thinking?"

Lance tapped the steel of the bed. It sounded like a hammer pinging on an anvil far away at the bottom of a deep well. The black turnip pulsed. It might be getting bigger.

"You should tell me where Laura is."

"Can'b youb fibe er?"

"No," Lance sort of said and sort of sighed, "she's a good person you see. The salt of the earth, as they say. And she doesn't want me to find her. That makes it hard. My, um, methods don't work so good against that. And then there's Rita. She's pretty strong. She doesn't really know what's going on, but she knows enough to push me off, push off my, um, searching."

"Bbbddd."

"Whatever. But you can tell me. You know where she is."

Happy was silent. The pulsing black onion was like a cloud, a deep dark storm cloud. Tiny glints of lightning were shooting out of it silently and washing across the bed, splashing down to the floor.

"I habe you. I habe you. Gob abway. Leeb be aloned."

"Then there's her mother, Cheryl, Cheryl McGovern. That woman's like an ox. She's got me shut down and out solid. I can't touch her. I can't get past her. I can't even start to deal with her. But you can just tell me."

"Aggbb! Aggbb!"

"Okay, okay, settle down, Happy. I'll go. You stay here"—the boy chuckled—"and get better."

Lance tapped the rail of the bed and seemed to move off.

Then Lance said from some distance across the room, heading maybe toward the door, "That Candy girl and her pimp—you don't have to worry about them anymore. They're dead. I killed both of them."

And just like that, the onion expanded like an utterly silent explosion, and Happy vanished from himself into the darkness.

7

County Prosecutor Dan Danovitch stood in the courthouse cafeteria with his tray squarely in front of him and scouted around for a batch of empty seats where he could eat. He liked to be alone when ate his lunch at work. He didn't like talking business; he liked getting away from the business for a little bit and having his own thoughts. His tray was a sad affair, decked with a large glass of water and a tiny plastic container of yogurt, a single napkin, and a single spoon. He was dieting; he was always dieting, and of course he didn't like it, but there it was. Finally he picked out six empty seats over toward the east windows, and he began maneuvering his way to get over there, picking his steps carefully between all the other courthouse diners. As he walked, Charles Rapp fell in step behind him, calling out, "Hey, Dan, let me lunch with you. I want to tell you about something." Dan sighed and grimaced; he wanted a silent meal but so much for that. He marched on toward the empty seats with a depressed spirit of resignation, but he knew he was exaggerating.

Charles Rapp was a career homicide detective, a somewhat portly sweaty man who took his job seriously, but no one would ever say he was obsessed with it. He was familiar with crime, and he studied it, but he kept it separate from himself; he had a detached expertise with murder; but even in the middle of the worst crimes imaginable, he kept himself, his real self, detached. It was as if he was only watching crime and investigation and prosecution, but he never let himself be absorbed in it. If he had something he wanted to share with Dan, it was probably a curiosity or oddity or even comic effect. It was unlikely that he would actually bother Dan.

They sat and began sorting and arranging their food, moving it off the trays. They would at least be civilized enough to eat off the table, not off their trays. It was a simple affair for Dan with just his yogurt and water but a bit more complicated for Charles. He had quite an array of dishes. It seemed that he liked to eat and that he liked to eat in the courthouse cafeteria, food that Dan hardly acknowledged as being actual food. Dan didn't know it, but this was basically Charles's one full meal of the day. Otherwise, he just snacked.

When they had their food all arranged and situated, Charles all at once became very still and slightly tilted his head forward. Dan wondered if he was having some kind of fit or something, but then he realized that Charles was asking for blessing on his food. Weird. Charles's head then bobbed up, and he grabbed his fork and started poking around in the mashed potatoes and gravy that took up one-third of his plate.

"How's Marie doing now, Dan? How are things working out for you, guys? And Mandy—is she recovering okay from that kidnapping and all that?"

Dan thought. What was the short answer to that? *Was* there a short answer?

Marie had been very nearly completely broken by Mandy being kidnapped. Dan had been afraid for her, afraid that as things might turn out, she would never recover. But once Mandy was almost magically saved, everything turned out differently than Dan could have ever have expected or hoped. By the time Mandy could visit her mother in the hospital, Marie had been through detox. She was unsteady and weak and little fuzzy in the thinking department, but for once, all the alcohol was out of her system. They held each other and cried and talked endlessly, Mandy describing over and over what had happened. This was a girl who had drifted into hardly talking to her mother at all for years, barely exchanging single words and only as necessary. Now they were pouring their hearts out to each other.

They decided, Marie first and then Mandy in time agreeing with her, that Mandy being saved from the kidnappers was an act of God. Dan backed away from that. He didn't have such a favorable impression of Lance that he would put him in the servants-of-God category, though maybe the boy was delusional and thought he was a servant of God. Marie said, "Well, certainly it's supernatural," and Dan could follow along with that even though he didn't quite believe in the supernatural. He just took *supernatural* as a word for *weirdly inexplicable* and agreed with Marie. More to the point, Marie and Mandy experienced this sudden supernatural act as a call to religion, and they answered the call with full and complete exuberance. If Marie wasn't at an AA meeting, discussing the rescuing grace of a higher power, she was on her knees at a prayer meeting, speaking directly to God, or at a study group, learning the word of God. For Mandy it was the same, though she wasn't attending AA but rather a group for teenage children of alcoholics. For Marie and Mandy, everything fit together; and everything was explained; and they had a clear path for fruitful and happy life, which was good, better than Dan had ever expected to see.

As for Dan, he made a real effort to get to at least one Al-anon meeting a week. He didn't go in much for the higher-power business or the semi-religious tone of the meetings, though that was harmless enough, but it was a great help for him to learn directly from other people's experience about alcoholism and the problems that emerged from trying to live with an alcoholic even if the alcoholic wasn't drinking anymore. On the family front, it seemed that his family was blossoming into full and happy recovery.

What was the short answer for that?

"They're both doing fine, just fine. They both got religion."

Charles gazed at Dan seriously and steadily.

"There's nothing wrong with religion, Dan."

Dan could feel the two of them right at the edge of a deep conversion lecture, a call for Dan to fall on his knees and accept Jesus into his heart. He shied away.

"No, no, of course not. I'm a church-going man myself. I think it's wonderful. It's really brought them peace . . . their religion . . . it's great."

Charles nodded with solemn seriousness.

"Well," and Charles dug in with his food, eating with avid industry, swinging his elbows as he shoved the beans and potatoes and roast beef around, steadily loading forkfuls into his mouth.

"So, Dan, I think this will interest you," Charles said between mouthfuls. "Lance Thompson—that boy who slaughtered all those guys in Henderson and saved your daughter, of course, you remember him."

"Of course."

"And you remember we did ballistics and all eight men and two women were killed with one head shot each with bullets that came from the same gun, right?"

Dan nodded.

"Okay. Then, what? Four days later? A guy up in Chicago who thinks he's Mr. Big in organized crime gets one bullet to the head right in the kitchen of his swank penthouse apartment. Ballistics goes through, and it's the same gun."

"Right."

"So in about four days, this boy wipes out eleven criminals, one of them major league, one of them minor league, and the rest thugs or whores."

"Uh-huh."

"So how do you figure this boy? Does he think he's some kind of caped crusader, a vigilante for justice, cleaning up Dodge City? What's the kid about, Dan?"

Dan had peeled back the thin plastic top from his yogurt, and while Charles had put away maybe half a pound of food, Dan had worked his way down to the fruit at the bottom of the cup. He guessed that you were supposed to mix the fruit into the yogurt, but he always just ate the yogurt down and then ate the fruit by itself, sort of as a tiny dessert.

"Yeah, I've thought about the kid. He's definitely a jerk, but is he a citizen gone wrong or a bad guy?"

Charles nodded, but his eyes narrowed as if he didn't quite get what Dan was talking about.

"Well," Charles said, "he apparently doesn't like, um, bad guys, but I think he's some kind of psychopath, a plain and simple mad killer, at root."

Dan laid his cup aside and took a drink of water to wash out the bright sugary fruit taste.

"You have anything new?"

Charles had slid his chocolate cake in front of him and was beginning to slice it with his fork, measuring off a good mix of frosting and cake for his first big bite. He paused.

"The other day, back behind Great Wall Chinese, shoved against a row of trash cans, we find a prostitute and her manager, each with one bullet to the head. I just got ballistics back, and it's the same gun, the boy Lance's gun."

They both sat still and let that stand.

"I don't get it, Dan. He wants to save the DA's daughter to keep his name clear, and he doesn't like the creeps who grabbed her, okay, and then he blasts some self-ordained dark drug lord of Chicago, yeah, yeah, I'm thinking crime-stopper killer with a big twisted ego. But a two-bit pimp and his nickel whore? I just don't get it. What's it about?"

"I don't know." Dan paused and looked away. Finally he said, "I think the boy has gone crazy. I think the boy has just gone crazy."

Charles charged back to eating his chocolate cake.

"Anything about the pimp and the whore? Who they saw, what they'd been doing?"

Charles waved his fork.

"Not much, Dan. There was a report that some private detective, one of those background-check guys, got beat up by the pimp. He's in pretty bad shape. Name of Happy Wilson. We questioned him, but we didn't get much. He's pretty confused. You got anything on the Thompson boy?"

"Well . . . I interviewed him, and a woman Michelle McKinney interviewed him. In fact, he was the last person she interviewed. She up and quit after talking to him. I think I'll see if I can find her."

Charles tilted his head and made a questioning face, raising his eyebrows.

"The county prosecutor is going to go out and do detective work?"

"Well, what with Mandy and all, I'm sort of personally interested."

"Whatever. I hope you find him but tell us. Don't go off hunting him down yourself and confronting him. Like you said, he's crazy. We can handle him."

"Right. I'll look for him a little and let you know if I find anything."

Charles nodded as Dan got up and walked off, carrying his tray. And Dan thought to himself, *If I find him, I'm going to kill him. I'm through with this bastard.* But he didn't say that to anyone—not yet.

Dan had done a spot of military service back when he was going through college. It seemed smart; it was more or less like police training, the discipline and weapons and all, and it was good physical conditioning. The ROTC money made it easier for his first wife, Allison, and their boys, Trevor and Alexander. He might not have stuck it out and graduated if it hadn't been for that extra money. He was horrified when he found out he actually had to go on active duty for two years. The war in the Middle East meant his country needed him. He did his time in the military police. Active duty wasn't much duty, and it certainly wasn't active; he'd never been so bored in his life. It was probably the death of his first marriage, but otherwise it wasn't much, not much at all. Except: he did learn to shoot, and he did learn that he had a natural gift for shooting. It was just easier for him than it was for the other guys. The way to hold the gun—the breathing, the sighting—it all came to him as if he was born for it. The higher command wanted to make him a sniper, but Dan had already figured out that he wanted to be on the courtroom end of law enforcement, not the shooting-guns end of it. The courtroom was safer, and it paid better, and it had political possibilities that he found more gratifying to his ambition than medals and trophies for hitting paper targets better than other guys. He'd never actually used his shooting ability, but as he pictured Lance Thompson running amok through the Midwest slaughtering bad guys all on his own initiative, Dan thought it might be time to finally cash in on his old gift.

Later that afternoon, Chance Anderson sat at the table in Interview Room Two, slouching down as if trying to make himself smaller. Dan Danovitch sat across from him, the table between them empty—no papers, no briefcase. There was no guard in the room. They were alone.

"I don't have to say anything, not one word, without my attorney here."

"No. That's right. You don't have to say anything."

Dan stood up and started pacing slowly around the room.

"In fact, I don't want you to say anything. I just want you to listen."

Chance sat very still. Dan continued pacing, moving toward one wall, pausing, turning slowly, and then pacing back toward the other wall, on and on while he talked.

"Now, Chance, you seem to have a gift for acquiring things, particularly guns, that may or may not be stolen."

Chance rumbled as if clearing his throat and getting ready to speak. Dan waved him quiet.

"We've got evidence enough to hold you and evidence enough to cause you trouble, and I think we've got evidence enough to convict you of at least receiving stolen property if not out and out stealing it yourself, but I don't want to talk about that."

Dan paused in his walking and talking and then moved on.

"I've got a shiny brown SUV. Almost bran' new. I usually park it in my garage just to be safe, even though there isn't much crime in my neighborhood out there in Wendell Acres. You know it?"

Dan glanced at Chance, but Chance didn't respond. He just sat there unmoving, staring straight ahead.

"I'll take that as a yes. You've probably helped yourself to more than a few things out there."

Here again Chance began to make noises like he was going to speak, but Dan waved him quiet.

"Here's the address of my house where my shiny brown SUV will be parked in the driveway," and Dan pulled a small envelope from his pocket and set it on the table. "Here's the address, and here's a key that won't start the motor but it *will* open the back tailgate."

Dan waited, but nothing happened. He continued walking and talking, "So like I say, I'm thinking that maybe for a week or so, I'll just park my SUV out in the driveway."

Another pause.

"I would like a rifle, Chance. I would like a rifle that came from nowhere. I'm not picky, but it has to be a high-powered rifle, and it has to have a decent scope on it. The important thing is that the rifle has to have nothing at all to do with me. It just needs to appear in the back of my SUV, sometime next week. Maybe twenty rounds of ammunition."

"You gonna do some law enforcement all on your own?"

Dan stopped and stared hard at Chance, and Chance fell silent.

"I'm going to do some shooting, Chance," Dan said levelly as he started walking again. "I'm going to do some shooting, but you don't know anything about that, and you don't need to know anything about that."

Dan stopped his pacing and looked at Chance squarely. Chance didn't move or speak. Dan started pacing again.

"So you take this envelope with the address and the key, and I'll let you go, let you out right now and drop all charges, erase this whole thing. You go out right now a free man, no more accusations, no more trial. All that's done and over."

Dan stopped.

"And somehow, from somewhere, I'm pretty sure a rifle with a decent scope and twenty rounds will appear in my SUV." Dan gestured vaguely and said, "If it doesn't . . . well, I know where to find you, and we can start all this up again right quick, okay?" Dan reached out toward Chance. "Now you get up, and let's get you out of here."

8

Happy Wilson sat in a wheelchair out on the patio of the Midwestern Jewel Rest and Recovery Facility. It was a good place to be. He was more or less in the sun, which suited the late-October cool conditions. He could sit and look and look and look some more. He didn't need to do anything, and most importantly he didn't need to think anything. Wrinkled dry leaves scooted along the brick and concrete patio, making a sweet crinkling noise. Some of them were plain brown, plain as paper bags; but others were brilliant and beautiful, sharp gold or deep-red flashes of color in the light that soothed him instead of irritating him. Almost everything irritated him, but the leaves were gentle and kind—almost kind.

Happy had nearly died when Lance said he had killed Cerise. It was unbelievable, an unbelievable evil, but Happy believed it. That Lance boy seemed capable of anything, though why in the world would he kill Cerise? It made no sense to Happy, and it was so wrong and so out of step with any goodness in the universe that all Happy wanted to do was vanish. And for a time, that's exactly what he did. It could have been years, but probably it was only about six hours, six hours in which the nurses and doctors apparently went crazy and stuck tubes in him and pumped blood and who knows what into him. Happy went under; he dove deep, and he disappeared from the normal average world. Or perhaps he didn't dive. He just was pulled, or pushed, by events just too horrible to navigate, or to even understand, way down into some unconscious nothingness of pure blackness—absolute darkness.

All the girl had done was talk to Happy. And now she was dead. It seemed as if merely talking to Happy was a death sentence. Happy felt a chill whenever he thought about it. But he tried not to think about it. He tried not to think about anything.

If he had been capable of speech when he first more or less woke up from Lance's visit, he would have said that his brain felt like there was a flat white pine board placed diagonally straight across the center of his mind. It twisted some, and it turned. It hurt some. Mostly it kept anything he tried to think about from connecting. He would have a thought that should have led to another thought, a tissue of sequential notions forming into a complex idea, but the board was in the way like a locked shut door. All the pieces of his thoughts would remain unhooked from one another and wash away without ever arriving at sense.

There was pain. There was pain that varied from a tiresome ache all over his body, but particularly in his head, to sharp shooting pains that crashed along the board blocking his mind and careened into the walls of the inside of his skull like hot metal. But the pain wasn't quite as bad, or nameless, as the general feeling of being inadequate to even the most basic grasp of understanding. Quite simply, he felt that his brain was broken, perhaps forever.

The scenery shifted. He was brought here by means of a timeless ride in an ambulance. He was laid in a bed in a ward with half a dozen other men in various states and degrees of mental incapacity. He gradually was able to eat fruit gelatin and drink soft drinks. The nurses wheeled him out to the patio and back and cheerfully told him about how much better he was getting and so quickly. He was recovering. In just a couple of days, he had recovered considerably.

But he still couldn't quite connect and think like a person. The shooting pains struck him less often, and the deep ache seemed more shallow, but thinking was a challenge that didn't seem worth the effort. He let the nurses roll him around, and he ate and drank when he was told to.

Rita McGovern was his first visitor. The nurse wheeled him out to a wide open lounge like an enormous living room dotted with bad lavender furniture, and there Rita was, standing and waiting to see him.

Her face flashed into something like horror and then eased down to mere distress when she got a good look at him. The nurse wheeled him to the edge of a couch, and Rita sat down.

Happy was terribly distressed at seeing Rita. Even without being able to think clearly, he knew that Rita was in danger just by being near him; and if he could have, he would have shouted, "Go away! Go away! And never come near me again!" The boy wanted Laura, and he knew about Rita, and he might be watching. He might be able to see.

Evidently Happy was making some kind of noise, if not shouting, "Go away!" because Rita became alarmed and began gently stroking Happy's arm, saying "It's okay. It's okay, Happy. Calm down. Just be still. Shh, hush, hush, it's okay," this last gentle and quiet.

Happy closed his eyes and sat still. Rita left her hand on Happy's arm, barely a touch.

"Listen, Happy. Someone is after Laura."

Happy opened his eyes wide and stared at Rita, nodding slowly, trying to say yes without stimulating a pain in his brain.

"You know?"

Happy nodded.

"Did you getting beat up have anything to do with this?"

Happy knew that it didn't. His being beat up had nothing to do with Lance, but he nodded just because it seemed right. Things were more complicated than just nodding could indicate. He couldn't explain, but the boy Lance had become relevant to his beating, sort of after the fact.

"Oh, Happy, I'm so sorry. You shouldn't have been pulled into this."

Happy could have nodded to that, but he sat still.

"Listen, Happy. We're taking care of Laura. I'm doing my part as best I can, which is something, and Mom, who is way stronger than me, is going all out to protect Laura. She has a plan. She knows what to do, and she's going to take care of it. I think it's going to be all right."

Happy didn't respond. He couldn't believe at this point anything was going to be all right.

"You just need to sit still and get well and don't worry about it. We—Mom knows what she's doing. Whoever is after Laura, they're not going to get her. And Mom is going to finish it for good. You just have to trust her."

Happy sat still.

"You can't know, Happy, but you have to believe," Rita said, and she moved her hand gently on his arm.

Happy nodded.

Happy's next visitor was Dan Danovitch. Happy was slouching down on the back patio, absorbing and taking in and slowly digesting mentally all there was to see. He focused on being quiet in his mind and enjoying the feeling, the suggestion of a feeling, that the plank in his head was beginning to dissolve.

"Mr. Wilson, there's someone to see you."

Happy slowly rotated his head toward one of the younger nurses, a quick efficient sort who seemed somewhat like a younger Laura, and said his first clear word in days, "What?"

She beamed hugely and patted him on the arm. "Listen to you! You're already talking again! That's wonderful!" She turned and smiled at the man beside her, a sort of legal-looking character dressed head to foot in brown. "Mr. Wilson's injuries made it impossible for him to speak clearly, but we knew he'd recover. He's doing really well!"

Then she turned back to Happy. "This is Dan Danovitch, Happy. He's the county prosecutor. You've heard of him, haven't you?"

Happy gazed mildly at Dan and finally said almost experimentally, "Hello. Have a seat."

"Wonderful!" the nurse gushed. "You're so good for Mr. Wilson, Mr. Danovitch! We should have had you come to visit days ago." The nurse gestured toward a chair, and Dan sat down. "I'll just leave you two gentlemen alone here so you can talk about your business uninterrupted. Happy, I'm going to go call Dr. Angstrom right now and tell him how great you're doing!" And with that, she strode off, dutiful and focused and efficient.

Dan watched her go and then turned to Happy. "Mr. Wilson—"

"Happy. You can call me Happy."

Dan nodded. "Okay then, Happy. Now"—and Dan cleared his throat even though it didn't need clearing—"I believe you might be able to help me. I'm looking for Lance Thompson, and I—"

"Kill him."

"Pardon?"

"Kill the little monster."

"Yes, well." Dan seemed to consider the idea.

"It won't do any good to arrest him. It won't do any good to try to control him. You've got to get rid of him. There was no reason in the world for him to kill Cerise. He'd kill anybody. I have no idea what he wants with Laura, but it can't be good. Nothing good can come from him."

Dan sat still. "Well . . . Happy . . . that was quite a speech for a guy I was told couldn't talk at all."

It was true. Happy was almost exhausted completely by saying just that much, though the feeling behind it might have been the really exhausting part. He could feel the board in his head solidifying, and he tried to quiet himself, to be still. He closed his eyes and struggled to empty his mind.

"I'm trying to put all this together," Dan said after pausing so Happy could rest, "and I've gotta say it doesn't make a whole lot of sense. You say Lance killed Cerise. Who would she be?"

"Prostitute."

"Ah. She's better known as Candy, but Cerise . . . that almost sounds like it could be her real name. We haven't found much in the way of records for her. A fairly invisible young woman. Did you know her well?"

Pause.

Happy opened his eyes and looked down at his hands, which were folded in his lap. He looked at them as if they belonged to someone else.

"I was in the park, just sitting and trying to figure things out. Like you. Trying to figure things out. She sat next to me and made a proposition, which I declined." Happy's brain was chugging along just fine. He impressed himself. "Then we got to talking. I liked her. Then she left. Later I found out—" and Happy closed his eyes and slowly shook his head.

"Did you see the boy?"

Happy looked directly at Dan. "Yes, yes, didn't I say that?"

Dan shook his head once.

"Well, I meant to say that. The boy showed up, and she took off one way, and he took off the other way. I was trying to talk to him, find out what he wanted."

"Okay. It seems he wants Laura."

"Why?"

Dan thought, *Why does he want Laura? or Why does it seem he wants Laura?*

"Do you know why he wants Laura?"

Happy shrugged. "He told me that Laura could help him. I don't know. I thought maybe she had information he wanted, but now I'm thinking . . . well, I don't know . . . but now I'm thinking maybe he wants her to be his mom somehow. He's a strange sort of creep. Partly boy, partly adult killer. Crazy."

"Laura used to work with us in investigation and prosecution, the law, though I didn't know her. Then her name was Michelle McKinney. Laura interviewed Lance and then quit her job and moved in with her sister. It turns out Laura was adopted. She went back to her given name after she quit."

Happy sat still and silent as if he hadn't listened to a word Dan had said.

Dan tried again, "I need to find the boy. And to find him, I need to figure out what runs him, what makes him go where he goes and do what he does."

The plank in Happy's head had completely disappeared. He looked at Dan as if lost in thought and then said, "Looking for Laura seems to run him now. He, what? He acts like he is owed Laura, as if Laura belongs to him somehow. He deserves her. And he seems to think once he gets with Laura, everything will be great. That's about all I know."

Dan nodded and stood up.

Happy looked up. "You will protect Laura and Rita, won't you?"

"Oh yes, oh yes. I won't let anything happen to them. They'll be safe, especially once I get Lance. And I am going to get him."

Happy smiled. "That would be sweet."

Dan reached out to shake Happy's hand, and Happy didn't respond, only smiled dimly; so Dan just patted his hand, saying, "You take it easy, Mr. Wilson. Everything is going to be okay. You just get well."

Happy nodded and then looked away into the trees.

Happy's last visitor of the day—it was a busy day for him—was Cheryl McGovern. Unlike the other two, Cheryl didn't seem to have much to say. A rather more surly nurse interrupted Happy as he gazed into the flowerbeds and trees, saying curtly, "You've got a visitor" and stomping off.

Cheryl stood and looked at Happy and then looked off in the direction he was looking.

"Nice," she said.

She pulled a lawn chair over next to his wheelchair, close enough to talk but not close enough to crowd, and sat herself down. They sat there quietly for a few minutes without moving. The air was comfortably cool, and the light was level and fine, touching the rough-to-smooth surfaces of the bark of the different species of trees, reflecting peacefully on the colored or bland leaves. It seemed a bit of peace, of paradise. Late insects buzzed by or merely floated, the careening swallowtails. A grasshopper departed in a whir of wings like a gentle small engine.

"Do you mind if I smoke?"

"No."

"Thank you. Most people most everywhere hate smoking like it was setting bombs off. I like it anyway. That's me."

Cheryl puffed on her cigarette and then held it out away from herself, turned parallel to her body. She might have been examining it, but the line of her sight never focused that close. She was taking in the broad scenery. It was late afternoon, and the day was beginning to look worn down, though the brightness of sunset and twilight were still ahead. It was as if the light was resting before the last rush of vividness and clarity.

"This is really nice, Happy. Really nice. You like just sitting out here looking at it all, don't you?"

Happy nodded and then quietly said, "It's beautiful. It heals me just to sit and look and not think about anything."

"I know exactly what you mean. People think we're put in this world to do all sorts of things, to work and to make things. But first of all, we're put here just to be here. Just to be here."

"I believe that."

"Well now," Cheryl said, more or less like a sigh, placing her hands on her knees, one pair of knuckles still holding the stub of her cigarette, "you're probably wondering who I am. I'm Cheryl McGovern, Happy. I'm Laura's mother. And Rita's mother."

Happy turned and looked at her, taking her in with the same peaceful attitude of observation he had been giving to the trees and flowers and light.

"I know your girls. They are waitresses at the Spotlite."

Cheryl nodded. "Yes." She paused and looked at Happy and then back at the landscape. "They're smart girls. They could do more and probably will do more. But serving people, taking care of people—that's a good job. The most important thing in the world to them is that they be together, and working at the Spotlite gives them that."

They sat quietly for a few minutes.

Turning to Happy, Cheryl said, "I'm mighty sorry that you got pulled into this whole Lance Thompson problem. You've been good to my girls, and you were good to Cerise. You connected with her when hardly anyone ever did. She told you her name. Her real name. You must have done more than you know for her to do that. That's something. That's a lot."

"You knew Cerise?"

"Some." Cheryl seemed to want to dismiss talking about her.

"Now listen, Happy. This Lance thing is reaching the point where it's all going to explode, which will be awful, but then it will be over. It will be over forever."

"That would be fine."

"It will be fine. But I think"—and Cheryl paused and tipped her head as if listening close to a small voice—"I think I'll be going away. You and Laura and Rita will be okay, but I think I'm going away."

"Oh? A new start somewhere else?"

"Yes, Happy," she said after sitting still for a moment, "that's pretty much it I think. A new start somewhere else. That's a good way to put it."

"I'm sorry to hear that."

Cheryl shrugged. "I'll be fine wherever I go. I just won't be here. But I've got a house on some country property I think you would like. It's a wonderful place to just sit and look. It's a great place to be. A garden, fields, some trees, a good view of a wood lot, quiet space, and nice light. I want you to have it. I want to sign it over to you. And I want you to have my investments, not much but some stocks and bonds, some money in the bank. Enough for you, I think."

At this she smiled and then looked directly at Happy.

"You okay with that? It would be a good place for you to heal and get whole."

"Yes. Yes. It's really not necessary. Shouldn't the girls—"

"The girls will be fine. I've taken care of them. This is for you. For Cerise. And for getting caught in the line of fire in a way you never should have been. A fellow will be out tomorrow with the papers. Don't try to understand them. Just look at them like you're reading and then sign where he tells you to. I'll tell the girls, and when I'm gone, they'll take you out there, get you the keys."

The stand of trees was beginning to flare up with the falling light of the day, angular smooth beams of illumination sorting between the bare trunks of poplars and sycamores.

"That sound okay to you, Happy?"

"That's fine. That's good. I don't deserve all this, you know."

Cheryl chuckled softly. "Oh yes, you do, son. Yes, you do. You don't know."

9

Dan Danovitch had just finished chatting with a confused citizen and his confusing legal help in Interview Room Number Three. It had gone okay, but it didn't give Dan much in the way of a sense of accomplishment. What people don't know. It was a puzzle to Dan how ignorant most of the citizens were—clueless cattle staggering around the corral, bumping into one another, and getting in trouble. As Dan headed back to his office, he wondered what to do now. It wasn't that he didn't have work to do. He had plenty of work to do. Having work to do wasn't a problem. He often reflected that if he worked 168 hours a week, he would never make a dent in all the work he could do. Reminding himself of that encouraged him to back off and not try to fill each day with too much. Marie and Mandy needed his time more than the county did. In the long run, he would get to what he needed to get to for the county, and the rest would just gradually fade away. His assistants, his stupid assistants, could actually handle almost all of it. And to hear them tell it, they did.

What puzzled Dan specifically was what to do next about Lance Thompson. He felt like he had found out as much as he could; what he knew now was as much as he could know under his own power. Mostly he just had to wait until something else slid out of the woodwork, but he was impatient. He wanted the thing done and over, finished.

He was startled to find a woman sitting in his office, but after a quick look at her, he decided it was okay. She looked like Buddha. Or Gertrude Stein. Sitting heavy and solid, a strong immovable mass utterly at peace with itself. She seemed about as threatening as a figure made of wood, an idol. Maybe dangerous to believers but Dan didn't even know who she was. He would sit—he did sit—and let her magic, whatever it was, reveal itself in its own time.

Cheryl McGovern had hitched a straight-backed chair up to Dan's desk, and she was gazing down into a book as if looking into a crystal ball. Dan recognized it at a glance; it was a book someone had just sent him, a book he hadn't read but he had thumbed through. That was why it was on the desk. It was called *The Problem of the Deviant Student in the Classroom*, and it was written in a fairly lame sort of psychobabble that might or might not actually say anything. It did have graphs and charts, so maybe there was something to it. Dan could reserve judgment just as he was reserving judgment on the pillar of Cheryl McGovern.

She looked up from the book as she closed it and said, "I'm Cheryl McGovern, Laura's mother, though maybe you know her better as Michelle McKinney."

They sat with the desk between them and sized each other up for a long minute.

"You know, Mr. Dan," Cheryl said, tapping the book, "I never had much use for school, with or without deviant students. It's great for arithmetic or learning the states and their capitals, but when it comes to finding out what you really need to know, I've found you're on your own."

"Well"—and Dan seemed to consider being on your own for a moment—"I think I've reached the end of my knowledge with this Lance Thompson. Can you help?"

Cheryl seemed to wince. "Not much, Mr. Dan, not much. I could tell you things you probably wouldn't believe, but those things don't really matter."

"Well, tell me something anyway."

"It's like this—" and Cheryl gazed up at the high windows. "For most people, life goes along, and you can see what you see, and you make the best choices you can, maybe. But you don't always know how things will turn out. You stop at the grocery for milk, and you slip in the parking lot and hurt yourself. You knew what you were doing when you stopped and got out of your car. You were going to get some milk, but you didn't see that you were going to break your leg. We move according to what we know, but we don't know much, not really. And things don't play out exactly as we expect them to or want them to."

"Your point?"

"Don't rush me, Mr. Dan," Cheryl said, turning to face him directly. "We need to understand each other. I generally talk like a hick, and I can talk like a hick right now, but I don't want to. I want to be absolutely clear with you. It's vitally important that you and I set out from here understanding each other. You have to know where we are here at square one, or we'll never get to the finish we both want. I'm trying to get across to you as best I can."

They looked at each other.

"Okay. Proceed."

"Everyone knows there's more to life than meets the eye. Even the cattle in the corral"—and Cheryl tipped her head toward Dan significantly, as if she had heard what he had been thinking earlier— "know there's more here than the surface. Most folks live as if the surface is all there is. They avoid the sensation of something being behind the facade. But everyone knows that there are connections the facade can't tell you enough about, connections hidden underneath. In fact, the surface of life is only one surface. There are many depths, Mr. Dan. The surfaces are like onion skins, and they just keep going down and down. That can give a person vertigo. People are afraid of it or they're irritated by it, but anyway they dismiss it. They call it chance or coincidence or synchronicity. They give it a name and pretend that they've solved it, and they don't need to think about it."

"Yes. Okay."

"Some of us are more sensitive to the deeper layers. Some of us are even attracted to looking deeper than what we can see. There's a wide variation in how deep people can see."

"Okay."

"We all act as best we can with the information we have. Some of us have more information than others, and some of us can even act beneath the surface, make things happen that don't seem possible to people who just want to stay on the surface. But just as you're not sure what's going to happen in normal life, just as you make your best guess with the best intentions on the surface of life, people who are in the depths can act and sometimes make mistakes. Waking up in the hospital with a broken leg when you just wanted to get some milk . . . that kind of thing can happen all the way down."

"Nobody knows everything."

Cheryl's face lit up in a brilliant smile, a flash of a grin and huge bright eyes, and then relaxed as she nodded. "That's excellent, Mr. Dan. We understand each other. 'Nobody knows everything.' That's exactly right. I'm pretty sure I know more than you do about the depth simply because I've looked directly at it more than you, but I can still make mistakes."

Dan waited.

"Do you mind if I smoke?"

"Yes, I do."

Cheryl grimaced. "Well, fine. We don't need to be entirely sympathetic to each other, I guess."

She ran her finger along her lips and glanced slowly around the room. Light was slanting in from the late-afternoon windows throwing bars across the bookcases full of law books, making a design that moved slowly across the floor.

"So. My girl Rita knew she was missing her sister. I was foolish enough to have given Laura up for adoption, but Rita was smart enough to know that she was missing something under the surface that belonged to her. It was tough for her, but life is tough for everyone. Then things started to go all wrong for the poor girl. Her husband and sons were killed in a car wreck, and she was damaged, really damaged."

Dan listened.

"You know, Mr. Dan, if you get really hurt, if your body gets badly smashed and you lose your purpose in life, like your being a wife and mom at the same time, well . . . it isn't just your body that gets damaged. You get broken inside. You can't get well. You can only get worse. It was like that for Rita. I was losing her, Mr. Dan."

Dan nodded. Cheryl remained quiet. Dan prodded her, "I see. I see. Go on."

"As best I could see, which is like thinking you need to stop for milk on the way home I guess, the best I could see was that I needed to get Laura back for her. It was the physical trauma of the injury and the mental trauma of losing her husband and sons—that was what was tearing her apart and dragging her down, but Laura, being together again with Laura, I thought that could save her."

"That was the gallon of milk you needed."

"Yes, Mr. Dan, yes."

"And Lance Thompson? He was you slipping in the parking lot and breaking your leg?"

"Hmm. Pretty much that's how I see it, though it was worse than that. I knew—don't ask me how. I couldn't explain it if I wanted to—but I knew that Lance could reach Laura and tell her about us and send her to us. I knew that could happen, and I put my, um, thought and effort behind the scenes toward making that happen."

"The boys Lance beat to death?"

"I didn't look close enough. Or I just couldn't see. I didn't know anything about Lance or Michelle, but I knew that for me to find Laura a boy would have to commit a crime. I accepted that. When those boys died, I knew I was in over my depth." Cheryl sighed deeply and sat very still.

"And then Cerise—" and now Cheryl was weeping softly, tears running down her cheeks though she didn't make any crying sound or make any movement at all, just sat with tears running down her face.

"You knew her?"

"Barely. She could connect more than most. She had some power. She found me when she was about ten, just walked up to the house and visited me as if it was the most natural thing in the world, which it was but not in a surface sense. I couldn't figure exactly where she was from or precisely who she was, but I knew she didn't have anything and her path . . . her path was not a good one. The only thing that little girl ever had was her life, and that boy took it from her for no reason, for no reason at all."

Dan extended a box of tissues toward Cheryl, and Cheryl eventually took it. She set it on the book of deviant children in the classroom, slowly pulled a tissue out, and began dabbing at her cheeks as if she were an automaton.

"I think the boy has sex issues," Dan volunteered. "He accused me of abusing my wife, some other things. I don't know. But Cerise was a, um, sex worker. I don't know."

"Sex. I don't know either, Mr. Dan. I think I've enjoyed sex as much as anyone, but it's just sex. Jelly roll is sweet, but it's just jelly roll. It's not the whole world. Why do people get so wound up over it? Why is it such a big deal?"

Cheryl put her tissue on the edge of the desk and shrugged away all that, all that sex.

"Cerise visited three times over a couple of years. Then she disappeared. I knew she needed help, but I had Rita's boys to tend to, and I couldn't quite connect with Cerise, not quite. We had the touch for each other, but we couldn't get tied no—not to help, no. I don't think so," and Cheryl sighed again. "I don't know, Mr. Dan. I just don't know. Maybe I could have done more for her. But I can't do anything for her now."

Cheryl sat still, collecting herself.

"Well then, Mr. Dan, I did what I did with what I knew. I got Laura and I saved Rita, I think. I think both the girls will be fine, as fine as we get to be in this life. And I think I've made amends to Happy."

Dan nodded. He didn't know what she had done with Happy, but he assumed it was good; he trusted Cheryl by now.

"Otherwise, I've made a mess of everything by calling out that Lance boy and turning him loose. It's a mess I—we . . . have to clean up. That boy is like a mad dog, and we have to put him down, Mr. Dan. We have to put him down."

"Yes. Yes, Ms. Cheryl."

In spite of it all, Cheryl smiled.

"You've got a gun, a rifle, and you can shoot?"

"Yes."

Cheryl took a paper from somewhere inside the folds of her clothes and placed it squarely in the center of Dan's desk. "Tomorrow midafternoon or so, you be at my place. This is the address. Bring your gun and your bullets, and let's finish this. Until then."

Dan said fine, but Cheryl was already up and out the door far quicker than he would have guessed such a solidly built woman could move.

Dan arrived at Cheryl's house shortly after two o'clock. He could barely see it from the road, but pulling up the drive, he came out of the mask of cypress trees and found a typical more or less sturdy country house surrounded by flowerbeds with a statue of a woman fixed exactly in the center of the front yard. Only when he saw the curl of smoke from her cigarette did he realize that it was Cheryl. Dan was nervous, but as was his habit, he covered his anxiety by being cool and efficient. Or, rather, by trying to appear cool and efficient.

"Hello, Ms. Cheryl," he called out even as he was striding to the back of his SUV, popping the hatch open and pulling out the long cloth case that held his rifle.

"You come on in here, Mr. Dan," Cheryl called as she disappeared into the front door of the house.

When Dan came in, she was seated square and solid behind a long wooden table that shined empty and polished in the dining room end of the general living room. Cheryl gestured toward the table, and Dan laid the gun case down.

"How are you today, Ms. Cheryl?"

A look of slight irritation crossed Cheryl's face, and she waved Dan's question away.

"Let's see what you've got."

Dan unzipped the bag and pulled the rifle out. The scope was already mounted on it. He had spent almost an hour fiddling with it this morning, and after thinking and looking and studying the instrument, he had finally decided to just let it be. He didn't want to have to mount it again after he got to Cheryl's. He pushed the bag off the table and laid the rifle down. He put the box of bullets next to it.

Cheryl stared at the gun impassively.

"Your great granddaddy use that gun at San Juan Hill?"

"Okay, okay"—Dan grimaced—"it's old, but it's a good gun. And I can shoot. All I need is one good look, and the boy is gone."

"Perhaps."

Dan was irritated. "Shooting the boy is my department, and I can handle it as long as I get a look. The question is, will the boy be here? How often does he appear?"

"He'll be here. Those the bullets?" Cheryl gestured toward the box of ammunition.

"No, Ms. Cheryl, I brought you a box of chocolates."

"Mr. Dan, you better get serious. You're in more than you know, and you don't know what's going to happen. This is a heavy thing I'm working through. Keep your sense and keep your focus."

Dan looked down. "I'm sorry, Ms. Cheryl."

Cheryl smiled for the first time. "I'm sorry, Mr. Dan. I just made a joke myself a minute ago. I'm just a bit flustered and a little worried."

"He's only a boy."

"Yes. That's part of it. I hate to think of killing a child, even a monster child."

"What I meant was, how difficult can it be? He won't know what hit him."

"It will be difficult, Mr. Dan. I can assure you of that. This isn't entirely what it seems to be. It won't be like shooting a bottle off a log."

Dan paused. "No."

"Did you ever actually kill anyone?"

Dan shook his head. "No."

"Well then, there's that too."

"This is exceptional, though. For Mandy, for Marie, for everyone who runs into the kid—he's just out of control."

"I understand that. But it's like I said about stopping for milk at the store. We think we know what we're doing according to the information we have, but nobody knows everything."

"Right. Nobody knows everything."

They both sighed. Cheryl sighed as if she were stretching her entire soul all the way through her body, but for Dan it was more of a surface gesture, a small yawn.

"Open that box and give me, um, three of those bullets."

Dan did as he was told and extended the bullets to Cheryl. She looked at them as if she hated them and then looked up to Dan with an inscrutable look as she took them from him. She rose, muttered "excuse me," and disappeared into what Dan assumed was the bathroom.

Dan pulled a rag from the gun bag and started wiping the rifle down as if polishing it was an essential feature of the ritual they had entered. Water was running. He wondered if Cheryl was taking a shower, now of all times. He started shoving bullets into the magazine.

Cheryl came out of the bathroom, walking slowly. She was holding the shells between the fingers of her left hand, carefully not touching the bronze bullet ends. "Take them bullets out, Mr. Dan. They won't do you any good."

Dan looked at her and then shrugged. "Just one of these will blow him across the field."

"Mr. Dan, trust me. Those bullets are not what you want. Take them out and put them back in the box."

So Dan did as he was told and sat in his chair, the empty gun across his legs.

Cheryl extended the three bullets to him. "Don't touch the ends, Mr. Dan. Don't touch them at all. Just take the shell and put it in the gun. Put all three in that gun, but don't touch the ends."

"What did you do to them?

"I urinated on them, Mr. Dan."

"What? What? What?" Dan spoke fast and staccato, lurching back.

"I peed on them."

Exasperated, Dan spit out, "I know what urinate means. Why did you pee on the bullets?"

Cheryl sighed. "It's a hunch, okay? But it's a good hunch. It feels right. The boy and I are connected at a very deep level. You're going to do a violence to him with a bullet, but that needs to include me, the physical me, if it's going to cut him all the way down so he's gone for good. And it's going to take me too, Mr. Dan. It's going to take all of me, all the way down. I used him, and now I've got to even it all out. Just trust me, okay?"

Dan grimaced with distaste.

"Well, Mr. Dan, maybe blood would work. I thought of that. Do you want me to go in there and cut myself?"

Dan sighed. "No, no, no, whatever you think will work is fine. Let's not be drawing blood from each other. This is fine."

So Dan put the bullets slowly and methodically into the gun, taking each carefully without touching the tip and clicking it into the magazine.

"If I get a good look, one is all I need."

"Yes, Mr. Dan, that's what I think. You'll get a good look, and one is all you'll need, but . . . it's best to be prepared for whatever. Nobody knows everything."

Dan nodded. He held his gun, now loaded.

"What's the plan?"

"You follow me."

They went back through the kitchen—which was unusually plain, nothing old lady about it at all, plain muslin curtains, everything put away—and they moved toward the back door but at the last minute turned off to narrow steep steps that led upstairs. From the outside, Dan wouldn't have guessed this house had an upstairs; but after following Cheryl's slow and steady climb, he arrived in a long narrow angled ceiling room with a single dormer window off to the south, the back of the house. A kitchen chair stood at the window.

"You plant yourself there."

Dan sat in the chair and looked out. The window was open, and the screen had been taken out. He looked out over the backyard and garden, and off in the near distance, he could see a mowed hay field and then a woodlot of tall maple and oak trees.

"If it's as usual, he'll just appear there at the end of the hay field, easing out of those lilacs and brush probably."

Dan lined up his rifle and stared through the sight, carefully focusing. The crosshairs drifted back and forth along the edge of the hay field as he shifted the rifle back and forth.

"You see that wood slat chair there at the end of the garden?"

Dan looked over the sight, lowering the gun. "Yes."

"That's where I'll be sitting. He'll appear and start walking toward me. You get him, right?"

"Right," and Dan squinted into the sight again.

"Now, Mr. Dan, you put your gun down, and you listen to me." Dan set the rifle on his legs and looked at Cheryl. She seemed old but vigorous, strong and yet worn. "Look over there at the rose of Sharon, those white flowers with the pink centers."

Dan looked along the line of her pointing.

"At the base of those flowers, there's a well with a concrete top. I split the concrete yesterday—don't ask me how—and there's a slot just big enough for you to drop in your rifle and your bullets and the case—everything. When it's done, you drop it all in that well."

Dan gave her a quizzical look. "Anyone can find that."

Cheryl shook her head. "No, Mr. Dan, anything you drop in there will be gone forever. Don't you worry about that. Just don't look in when you drop it. There will be some, um, sparks."

"And the boy's body?"

Cheryl pursed her lips. "As I see it, you won't have to worry about that. But nobody knows everything. If there's a body, you'll have to take care of that."

"There will be a body."

"Maybe."

They looked at each other.

"Now listen. I'll be gone, okay? Don't worry about that. Happy Wilson will be taking over the place. It will be fine."

"The detective?"

"Yes, the detective. We've got that all settled. Get the gun in the well and do it without touching the bullets . . . if there are any left."

"I only need one shot."

"Yes, I think so, but put it all in the well. Now I'm going to go and sit, and we wait."

"Does he come every day? Are you sure he'll come?"

"No, he doesn't come every day. He's only been here maybe three times, three times that I knew about. I doubt he could have been here without me knowing, but—"

Dan glared. "Three times? That's all? Only three times? Then how do you know he'll be here today?"

Cheryl looked at Dan steadily for a moment. "Because I'm calling him, Mr. Dan. I'm calling him. He's coming. You can be sure he's on his way, and he'll be here."

And with that, Cheryl walked off and headed down the steps. A few minutes later, he saw her emerge into the backyard and walk with steady calm and grace out to the slat wood chair. She swung herself down lightly and seemed to all at once freeze into complete stillness. From where Dan was, looking at Cheryl was like looking at the back of a statue of Buddha.

Dan found an old blanket, folded it into a tight fat square, and placed it on the windowsill. He pushed aside the chair, sat down on the floor, and rested the rifle on the blanket. Peering through the sight, he moved the crosshairs in a slow sweeping motion back and forth along the edge of the hay field. This would be fine. Now all he could do is watch and wait. Cheryl remained perfectly still, a small dark figure squatting almost at the end of the garden. Dan watched. A slight trail of smoke rose from Cheryl's right hand. After she finished her cigarette, she flipped it away into the grass; and then she just sat, absolutely still.

Nothing happened. For long minutes and then for half an hour, nothing happened. Birds dipped down to the surface of the pond, eating at the insects, sometimes splashing the water and making bright circles stretch and widen across the water, falling gradually still. Insects chirred and buzzed. The flowers stood still. The long tall trees with their handsome brightly colored leaves simply stood still.

Dan tried to watch with a wide gaze, taking in everything at once. Then he worked his way across each thing he could see, focusing on each slight detail. Then he went back to a general look at the whole scene. He shifted back and forth in his vision, the general to the specific and back, his eyes always moving; but he never moved his body. Then he would force himself to move, force himself to change position a little bit, stretching his arms and legs in small degrees just to keep from tightening up.

Nothing happened.

Then Dan noticed that Cheryl slightly inclined her head, just the smallest motion of tilting her head forward, away from Dan. Instantly Dan was alert, scouting with his eyes along the brush and lilacs at the edge of the hay field. Nothing.

He glanced back at Cheryl, and he was startled almost into crying out by the boy, walking slowly behind Cheryl, approaching her from her left, over her shoulder. He was moving from the house toward Cheryl's back. Lance seemed to be reaching out toward her, extending his hand toward her. Cheryl did not move.

Dan swept the gun down and pointed directly at the back of the boy's skull and fired. The blast of the gun was followed by an immediate much louder explosion like a burst of the thunder; and a searing hot light erupted like a flash of lightning, stretching from the boy to Cheryl, an arc of impossibly bright light.

Dan fell back into the room, blinded and burned, his face and hands blazing and stinging as if with a terrible acid. He rolled over and over, crying out in pain, crying, "Jesus! Jesus! Sweet Jesus! Sweet Jesus!" But the pain quickly passed from his hands and face. He had his eyes clenched shut, and he could only barely open them, slowly relaxing against the sting; but it was easing. The sting was easing. Dan stretched still, gasping a little for air, holding himself still, and forcing calm.

Finally pulling himself together, Dan crawled across the floor, edged up, and looked out the window. Everything was as it was before, though there was no sound—no birds and no insects. The scene was tranquil and quiet, the flowers and the shrubs, the tired spent garden, the far trees with their blocks of colorful leaves. The only thing changed was that where the boy Lance had been moving toward Cheryl, there was a small pile of smoking ash. And where Cheryl had sat so still in her slat wood chair, there was nothing but ash, smoking white ash, blowing away in a sudden breeze.

Cheryl had told him she would be gone. Cheryl had said disposing of the boy would take all of her, but Dan never guessed just what she meant. And he never guessed how much it would take out of him. Suddenly weak beyond merely the surface burns, he sat abruptly down, hard, on the chair he had been meant to shoot from. All of it swam through his mind: the terrible boy who had to go, the evil of that, of killing anyone, but the boy out of control and how violent he was, how in some part he meant good but served death. Cheryl's strength and solid easy grace, her understanding and love of life, all that traded in for this settling . . . of what?

So Happy Wilson would inherit paradise. And Laura and Rita would go on with their lives, twins finding their way with each other's comfort and help. Mandy and Marie, praying, as Dan would pray now . . . as Dan did pray now, asking someone, a higher power, sure a higher power, there must be a higher power, maybe even Jesus, for the good grace to accept and let go, to not try to control, to leave violence, all violence, alone, and walk at peace in the beautiful world.

He would never forgive himself, not completely. But that was essential. That was good.

And there would always be Cheryl McGovern—always and never again.